THE FIENDISH FOE AND THE DEADLY JEWELS

A POINT MUSE COZY PARANORMAL MYSTERY
BOOK 7

KELLY ETHAN

Copyright © 2022 Kelly Bowerman writing as Kelly Ethan.

All Rights Reserved.

This book and all its contents are protected by copyright law. No part of this publication may be reproduced, distributed, or transmitted in any form or by any means, including photocopying, recording, or other electronic or mechanical methods, without the prior written permission of the publisher, except in the case of brief quotations used in reviews or other non-commercial uses permitted by copyright law.

For permission requests, please contact:

Kelly Bowerman writing as Kelly Ethan

9 West Street, Campbell Town, Tasmania, AUSTRALIA

Email: kelly@kellyethan.com

Publisher's Note: This is a work of fiction. Names, characters, places, and incidents are a product of the author's imagination. Locales and public names are sometimes used for atmospheric purposes. Any resemblance to actual people, living or dead, or to businesses, companies, events, institutions, or locales is completely coincidental.

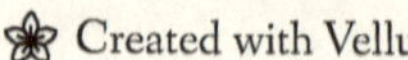 Created with Vellum

*A shout out to all those that have helped me with this series.
You rock!!*

THE FIENDISH FOE AND THE DEADLY JEWELS

A POINT MUSE COZY PARANORMAL MYSTERY BOOK 7

There's murder at the fun fair, a fiendish foe on the loose, and a nosy librarian turned sleuth. Let the mayhem begin...

It starts with karaoke and ends with murder. Xandie Meyers, librarian to the Supernatural Great Library of Alexandria, rued the day her grandmother, Elspeth Harrow, joined in Xandie's wedding preparations...with a karaoke engagement party.

Suddenly her police chief fiancé's bitter cousins are stalking Xandie, her jeweler won't give back her engagement ring, and she's been drafted into volunteering at the Point Muse fun fair.

The last thing she needs is for the fun fair to turn fatal and every finger points to the recently engaged librarian.

Xandie has no choice but to swing into Sherlock librarian mode and deal with the twisted carnival mayhem...

If you like snarky dialogue, murder and mayhem then you'll love the next installment in Kelly Ethan's Point Muse Cozy Paranormal Mystery series.

<u>Unlock the mayhem of The Fiendish Foe and the Deadly Jewels!</u>

ONE

"What's that old saying? You're not paranoid if they're really out to get you?" Xandie Meyers' neck itched. She spun and faced her stalker.

The figure darted into the dark alcove of a store that faced Main Street, Point Muse, home to the *Heart's Delight* bakery and the Supernatural Great Library of Alexandria. Easing a hooded head out before jerking back into the shadows.

"Yeah, my dame's stalking skills sure need some work." Colin, the talking pug, drew to a halt at Xandie's feet.

"Do I want to know why my wicked witch grandmother is stalking me through town?" Main Street and the whole of Point Muse sat on a nexus of ley lines and attracted magical creatures from all over the world. As Librarian to *the* supernatural Library, Xandie had all the handy statistics. What she didn't know was why Elspeth Harrow currently lurked in a doorway, watching her.

"Maybe she's looking for her marbles? Or it could have something to do with him." He jerked his head toward another figure scuttling across the road and disappearing into the alley behind her cousin Lila's bakery.

"Zach?"

"Your sneaky, sweaty, planning-evil-misdeeds boyfriend?" Elspeth sidled up to Xandie. "He's up to no good."

"Evil misdeeds? Zach Braun? He's a police chief. I'm pretty sure planning evil misdeeds isn't in his job description." If anyone was plotting, it was more likely to be a Harrow, and in particular, Elspeth.

"He's won't even look me in the eye. Classic signs of a guilty conscience."

"Maybe he *is* avoiding you. I know I do," Xandie muttered.

Elspeth waggled a fuchsia-tipped finger at her granddaughter. "I heard that. You're not too old that I can't hex your underwear drawer shut and leave you with your laundry day panties."

Xandie backtracked. "Maybe he had something else important to do."

Colin collapsed on the ground at Elspeth's feet. "Maybe he had a powerful urge for bakery leftovers. I could go a snack."

"He's up to something. I'll ferret it out. No one has secrets but me."

"Alright then." Elspeth's paranoia stemmed from the fact Zach had refused to talk to her. Every Harrow had wished upon occasion for the inability to hear Elspeth. "I'm heading into the bakery for lunch. You two can lurk as long as it's away from me."

"Hey, library girl. Wait up. I need refueling if we have to stalk you and your hot stuff any longer." Colin shook himself and padded after Xandie.

"I'll lurk in the shadows. That bear shifter will never know what hit him." Elspeth took a step and blended in with the shadows of the building.

"At least she has that creepy shadow thing down pat." Xandie held the bakery door open. Her cousin Lila's bakery was filled with eager customers munching on delicious-looking baked goods. And that included her still sweaty boyfriend, who hovered behind the counter as Lila handed over a bulging paper bag. Xandie raised a hand to wave, but Zach ducked into the kitchen without a second glance.

"You think a copper would have sharper covert skills." Colin slid past Xandie, making a beeline for the kitchen.

"That one, always thinking of his stomach. One day, it will explode." Holly popped up behind her cousin as Xandie waited in line at the counter.

"Probably." Xandie stared, distracted, at the swinging kitchen door that Hester, Lila's Brownie employee, had just popped back out through. She trusted Zach completely, but he did look overly sweaty and furtive.

Xandie stepped up to the counter where Hester and Lila stood, taking orders.

Lila flashed Xandie a distracted smile. "Busy today. What can I get my favorite Librarian?"

"Hot chocolate, please." Xandie tapped her short nails on the counter. "What's Zach doing? He told me he was flat out at the station today."

"Oh, he just came in to get some honey buns. He raced right back."

Hester snorted and restocked the glass cabinet with more baked goods.

Lila shot her employee a warning glance. "Sorry, no hot chocolate today. My machine's broken."

"Ah, man." Xandie pouted. "Okay, I'll have a brownie then."

"Again, sorry. I had a rush order. No brownies for you."

"I'll just have this, I guess." Xandie grabbed a small orange cupcake from a pile of food offered for free on the counter.

"No." Holly slapped the cake out of Xandie's hand. It dropped to the floor and Holly used her foot to crush it into crumbs.

Xandie and Lila stared openmouthed at their younger cousin.

"I saw bugs on it. You could have swallowed them and then they would have laid eggs. I saved your life. You're welcome." Holly blinked rapidly.

Xandie looked from her hand to the floor, then back to her cousins.

Holly patted Xandie's back. "Never mind. Why don't I take you home on my moped? The Library probably has something yummy waiting for you."

Xandie let Holly tow her outside to the waiting silver moped. "Since when do you offer rides? After Lila, you swore no one would ever sit their bottom on your moped but you."

"That's because Lila complained about my speed. I just like to be safe." Holly shoved a helmet at Xandie's. "Plus, you've never complained about my driving, *and* you won't say a word now." Holly climbed onto her moped but stiffened when she spotted a moving shadow. "Why is Elspeth playing hide and seek on Main Street?"

"She thinks Zach has a secret, so she's stalking both of us to unearth it."

"Typical. Always spoiling the moment," Holly muttered.

"Excuse me?"

Ignoring her cousin, Holly gunned her moped and took off...at a snail's pace. The girls both stared at their grandmother as they slowly passed. Elspeth Harrow peered out from the shadows, amber eyes gleaming as the girls drove past. At least her grandmother wasn't bored. Bad things happen when a Harrow was bored.

The moped shivered and rumbled under Xandie, and she grabbed Holly tight around the waist. Then the moped jerked and bucked and came to a shuddering halt just before Mayweather Inn.

"Hecate's cursed engines," Holly swore and yanked off her helmet. Muttering under her breath, she gave the machine a swift kick.

"I take it that's not good cursing?" Xandie removed her own helmet and stood next to the swearing banshee.

Holly glared at her moped. "No issues until I offer to drop the Librarian home. What are the odds?"

Xandie offered the helmet to her cousin. "I'm close enough to the Library I can walk home. Or I can always call Zack."

"No," Holly shrieked. "If you cut through the rose garden at the side of the inn, you'll get home quicker. I'll stay here."

"Why? Just leave the moped here. We can both go to the Inn."

Holly stepped closer to her moped. "It's Point Muse. Who knows what might happen to my silver baby? Just go through the rose garden and send someone back. It'll be fine."

Looks like it wasn't just Elspeth losing their marbles. "Okay. I guess." Sighing, Xandie walked toward the Inn. Coming to a small wooden gate, Xandie let herself into a pretty garden. "Rose Mayweather might hate all Harrows, but she plants a beautiful garden."

The sudden loud clearing of a throat shocked her. She peered around and spied her boyfriend, Zach, sitting on a bright red blanket with a bulging picnic hamper next to him. "Zach?"

The bear shifter stood and smoothed his palms along with jeans. "I thought I'd surprise you with lunch."

That's why he'd been lurking around the bakery. Lila probably filled the hamper with baked goodies. And that also explained Holly's weird slapping of the cupcake. "So, Holly's breakdown was a fake?" She eyed her boyfriend.

"She offered to get you here." He swallowed. "We had a hard time shaking Elspeth off our tails. She's been stalking me."

Xandie settled on the blanket next to Zach. "Elspeth thought you were up to no good. She hates secrets unless they're hers."

"It's almost over, then I won't have to worry about her, anyway."

"You planning on taking out my grandmother and burying her in Mayweather Inn's rose garden?"

"What?" Zach's eyes widened. "No. I-I." He stuttered to a stop and took a deep breath. "Why don't we have lunch?" He slipped a hand into the picnic basket without looking. Out of the blue, he shrieked and jerked his hand back.

Xandie winced. "Is there an issue? An Elspeth booby-trapped picnic?"

"Worse." Zach pointed at the basket. A food-smeared Colin, the pug, squeezed his head out.

"Hey, I'm stuck. You might need to cut me out. I think it

was that last mouthful of chocolate mousse. It seemed crunchy."

"*Noooo*," Zach bellowed and tugged at the pug.

"Um, Zach?"

"Hang on. It'll be fine. He couldn't have eaten..." Zach tugged hard, and Colin tumbled out onto the picnic blanket. Ignoring the dog, the bear shifter rummaged through the basket. "*No. No. No.* You ate everything."

Colin wobbled as he stood, a green tinge to his furry face.

"Ah, sweetie?" Xandie tried again. "Colin looks like—"

Zach held a hand up as he searched the basket, dumping half eaten containers on the ground.

Colin suddenly threw up over the picnic blanket next to Zach.

"Never mind." Xandie shook her head.

"This is all Elspeth's fault." Zach grabbed a stick from the garden and picked through Colin's puddle of reconstituted food.

Standing and moving backward, Xandie tripped over a half-eaten container of chocolate mousse. She picked it up and looked inside to find a large ring with an amber stone dead-center in the mousse. Plucking it out, Xandie cleaned off the dessert. The ring had flowers etched along the silver band and the amber stone stood out loud and proud in the center. She glanced over at her boyfriend, who now had Colin upside down, shaking him.

"Aha." Elspeth burst out of a rosebush. "I knew it. A dog napping fiend."

"What?" Zach paused, and both man and dog stared at Elspeth.

She pointed a shaking finger at the vomit puddle on the blanket. "And you've been torturing him?"

Zach raised his eyebrows. "Why would anyone kidnap this walking garbage disposal?

"Sweet cheeks?" Colin now rested against Zach's chest. "I stowed away in the picnic basket and ate all their food."

"Oh." Elspeth deflated. "That's different, I guess. But there's still vomit on the ground."

Zach cleared his throat and held Colin under his arm. "I shook him. I thought he might have eaten something important." Zach knelt next to the vomit puddle and poked around in it with a stick, mumbling to himself.

"Something like this?" Xandie held up the ring sans mousse.

Freezing like a deer in headlights, Zach paled and swallowed a few times.

"That's why he's been so sweaty." Elspeth clapped her hands and cackled.

Sometimes a girl's gotta do things for herself. "Zach Braun, will you marry me?" She winked at her silent boyfriend.

"It would be my honor, Xandie Meyers, to marry you." Zach dropped Colin to the ground and stepped over the vomit puddle. "This isn't exactly the way I wanted the proposal to go." Zach leaned in for a kiss which Xandie sidestepped.

"No offence, but you were just searching through vomit with a stick. I'm happy to take a rain check on the newly engaged celebratory kiss until we're certain you didn't get anything gross splashed up onto your fingers."

Zach smiled wryly. "I guess this is the way my life goes now. Chaos, mayhem, and dog vomit."

Elspeth snorted. "Don't forget a dead body or three."

Xandie smiled and slid the ring onto her finger. "No proposal is complete without a wicked witch grandmother."

Xandie wouldn't have any other way...

TWO

"What fresh hell is this?" Alexandra Meyers, a.k.a. Xandie, Librarian to the Supernatural Great Library of Alexandria, moaned and lowered her head into her hands.

"This is what comes of letting a wicked witch join in wedding planning." Lila Harrow, Xandie's cousin, flicked a long, brown, curly lock over one shoulder and smirked at her despondent cousin.

Xandie lifted her head and glared, amber eyes narrowing on the mouthy baker witch. "Let her? You think I had a choice? She threatened me with a hex worse than death if I didn't let her plan my engagement party."

"She threatened your underwear drawer again, didn't she?" Holly, the youngest of the trio of Harrow cousins, popped a small handmade chocolate into her mouth. "Those Devlins have a touch for sinful desserts for sure."

"I still don't like them." Xandie glared at the twin witches.

"They're still flirting with your soon-to-be-deafened-by-karaoke fiancé?" Lila shoved a small orange cake into her mouth and closed her amber eyes. "I nailed that orange boost-your-confidence cupcake."

Xandie rolled her eyes and sighed. Her eldest cousin – by a few weeks – poured all her witchy Harrow gifts into her baked goods and bakery, Hearts Delight. Lila's customers always left with a spring in their step, depending on which baked goods they'd consumed. Unfortunately, no amount of boost-your-confidence cake would save the disaster unfolding in front of her. Elspeth had set up a large screen and a microphone, along with a small stage, at the back of Harrow House grounds. She'd laid out tables and chairs, put down the dance floor, invited half the town of Point Muse, and whipped up barrels of her lethal Witchshine. The wicked witch matriarch of the Harrow family thrived on chaos and mayhem and possibly an odd virgin or two. So, karaoke fit right in with the wicked witch's love of mayhem.

Xandie winced as her mouthy feline, Theo, immortal guardian to the Supernatural Great Library of Alexandria, hit a viciously high note in his rendition of an angsty power ballad. "I regret the day he found his voice."

"More accurately, when Elspeth spelled him to sing. You know she has a thing about that Celine Dion song." Holly shuddered, and her eyes glazed over as Theo trilled a piercing high note.

Xandie slumped in her chair. Surely her life couldn't get any worse?

"I'm a hit." Elspeth appeared out of the dark, beaming at her granddaughters. "I knew all you naysayers were wrong. Karaoke *is* the ultimate icebreaker. Perfect for an engagement party."

"Perfect in what twisted, bizarro world?" The words popped out of Xandie's mouth before her brain engaged.

Elspeth's gaze narrowed on her newly engaged grand-daughter. "Suck it up and play nice, or all that new lacy underwear you paid a pretty penny for has a date with an itching hex."

Xandie swallowed heavily and forced a weak smile. Elspeth Harrow, the wicked witch of Point Muse, never made a threat she couldn't follow through on. And the matriarch of the Harrow family had come prepared for any kind of action. The always-lie-about-your-age pensioner was obsessed with wigs and tonight had slapped on a vibrant, neon blue mullet. She paired the offense against fashion with a black and silver sparkling jogging suit with square shoulder pads. The chaos loving witch was ready to rumble. "I like the shoulder pads. It makes you look mean."

Beaming, Elspeth patted the frazzled Librarian on the cheek. "What a sweet thing to say to your grandmother. Now I'm off down to the gate. Apparently, we have gate-crashers. You mingle." She pointed a fuchsia-tipped nail at the cousins and disappeared back into the shadows.

"I hate how she does that." Holly stared morosely after their grandmother. "She used to step out of the shadows when I was a kid and scare me. Every day was a Halloween scare."

Lila flicked a finger against her cousin's forehead. "That's because you used to raid her chocolate stash."

"Hey," Holly protested. "I was saving her future denture bills. She should be grateful." Holly grabbed her throat. "I think I'm getting a cold. Super sore throat." She jerked her head at Lila. "Do I have a temperature? Will that get me out of karaoke?"

Lila reared back. "Keep your cold to yourself, even if they are pretend germs. And nothing gets us out of karaoke."

Xandie held up her frizzy shoulder-length brown hair and massaged the back of her neck. "Can we please talk about the elephant in the room?"

"Technically, we're outside, not in a room," Lila offered with a wink.

"And Elspeth isn't an elephant, more like a rabid Chihuahua with wicked tendencies." Holly glanced around. "She didn't hear me say that, did she? I'm the only single one here. I need access to my underwear drawer more than you two do."

"Argh." Xandie closed her eyes and slid down until her face lay on the tabletop. Elspeth had gone all out for the karaoke engagement party. Soft, white, embroidered table-cloths covered the tables which were dotted around the back lawn of Harrow House. The small stage stood near Elspeth's Witchshine shed, and she'd set up a keg with a tap. The food tables were lined up on Harrow House's back porch with different themed stations of flavorsome offerings. The house made sure light blazed out of every window, lighting up the festivities. Harrow House had served gener-ations of witchy Harrows, and their powers had sparked the house's sentience. Now the black and purple Victorian resi-dence was just as opinionated and stubborn as every witch who resided inside. Including the matriarch, Elspeth Harrow.

"Let me guess. Elspeth paranoia?" Miranda Harrow slid into a chair next to her daughter.

Cracking an eye open, Xandie glared at her mother. "It isn't paranoia if they're truly out to get you."

Smirking, Xandie's mother gestured over her sullen daughter's head. "Nicolas. Come deal with your daughter. She's obsessing over the possibility of Harrow-caused mayhem." Frizzy brown hair streaked with silver hung just below Miranda's shoulders. Amber colored eyes identical to the rest of the Harrow family twinkled.

Tall, with silver-streaked black hair, Nicolas Meyers, Xandie's father, casually strolled to the table. Adjusting his tie with an elegant fastidiousness, he arched an eyebrow. "What did you expect when you agreed to an Elspeth-planned engagement party? You're lucky your guests aren't on some sort of energy draining psychedelic trip."

Lifting her head, Xandie gritted her teeth as she forced words out. "I. Did. Not. Agree. To. Karaoke." She groaned again. "This was a special surprise for me...*apparently.*"

Nicolas grimaced. "I did warn you about Point Muse. But you're as stubborn as your mother." He pressed a hand to Miranda's shoulder.

Her mother rested her head back against her husband's hand and smiled. Miranda Harrow had disappeared when Xandie was a little girl after being chased off a cliff by a killer knight. Suffering from amnesia, Xandie's mother had been trained as a black ops agent, hunting supernatural creatures. Eventually, she had regained her memories and settled back into Point Muse life. Unfortunately, Nicolas Meyers hated anything to do with the town, so Miranda had to commute between Point Muse and Andrews, the small college town where Xandie's dad lived and worked.

"Just another thing we all inherited from Elspeth. Stubbornness, snark, and amber eyes." All the family had the same eyes. Something to do with their witchy Harrow gifts. Lila, the eldest Harrow cousin, stood at five feet seven, with long curly brown hair and rocked an awesome witchy baking gift. She was also the most outspoken and their resident drama queen.

Xandie, the middle cousin, stood at five and half feet and had frizzy, shoulder-length, brown hair that she struggled with. She had a bookish bent, an obsession with sugar, and tended to leap before she looked. Holly, the youngest of the trio, although sharing the amber eyes, was the quietest. The banshee witch hybrid sported a smooth chin length brown bob and stood just over five feet. She worked at the local funeral home and preferred a good plan before leaping into action.

Holly noticed Xandie staring and wiped her chin self-consciously. "What? Do I have food on my face? Do I have a rash? Am I going to get sick and miss karaoke?" She swept a hand over her mouth. "Stop it. I'll tell Mom you're being mean."

"Whiner baby," Lila coughed into a hand.

"Now, dear. No whining at your cousin's engagement party. You'll never catch a boyfriend with that surly face." Winifred, Holly's mother and Miranda's youngest sister, waltzed past the table, keeping a firm hold on Caleb Braun's arm, Xandie's fiancé's youngest brother and a Point Muse deputy.

The tall, blond-haired man shot a frantic look at Xandie as the red-haired Winifred dragged the younger man around the dance floor.

Lila gave her aunt a thumbs up, then smirked at the deputy's discomfort.

With a stifled snicker, Xandie sat up. "See? Just like Elspeth. You delight in that poor young man's embarrassment."

"That young man is a heavily muscled bear shifter, who could shove his way through a brick wall. If he can't deal with Winifred on a dancing rampage, he shouldn't be a deputy." Lila poked her tongue out at her cousin.

Xandie tapped her fingers on the table. "It isn't just Elspeth and Winifred's karaoke shenanigans. Some of

Zach's family turned up from Germany. They live in the Black Forest. The German Brauns don't exactly approve of a shifter marrying a witch, especially a Harrow one."

Miranda stood and whispered a featherlight kiss over her daughter's cheek. "My offer stands. They'd never find the bodies." She linked hands with her husband. "If you will excuse us, we have some revenge waltzing to partake in." Xandie's parental duo wandered off to the dance floor.

"Do I want to know what revenge waltzing is?" Matthew Grim, Lila's boyfriend and the town reaper, dropped into a chair next to his girlfriend.

"Winifred bet twenty-four hours of Elspeth free time that she could take double the amount of turns around the dance floor as her sisters could. Now it's a marathon waltz to see who comes out on top." Holly shrugged. "It keeps their matchmaking mitts off me, so I'm all for parental one-upmanship."

Xandie peered around the back yard. "The Devlins have finally stopped monopolizing Zach. Any idea where he disappeared to?"

Matthew's gray eyes twinkled. "Feeling slightly anxious, are we?"

"When the chaos hits the fan, I want him to suffer just like I will. Share and share alike."

"Share? Funny word coming from a Harrow witch." A tall, heavily muscled young woman, with dead-straight, mousy brown hair parted down the middle, glared at Xandie. "The American branch of the family doesn't recognize the word. I shouldn't be surprised his fiancée doesn't either."

"This is Sofie Braun, Zach's cousin from the Black Forest." Xandie performed the introduction with a sigh.

Lila beamed at the woman. "German, right? Your

English is so clear. I've seen bloody family feuds started when one person couldn't understand the other. We're so lucky that isn't the case here." Lila clapped her hands in over-the-top delight.

Holly winked at Xandie and joined in with her own little hand clap. "Yeah, I mean, people can be so unpredictable when they don't understand what's going on around them."

Sofie glared at the banshee. "Are you calling me stupid?"

"Now, sister. These witches would not dare. They know strong German shifters are due respect."

Eric, Sofie's elder brother, muscled his way up to the table and handed his sister a plate heavily laden with food. "You must keep your energy up for the long trip back when we take our prized heirloom home."

Smiling sweetly, Sofie hefted the plate filled with creamy lobster pasta and butter sauce high. "Of course. I wasn't thinking, Eric. It's been a delight visiting with our country cousins, but we must be back home with our rightful inheritance. "

Xandie groaned mentally and thanked Hecate, the goddess of magic, that Elspeth or Aggie, Zach's mother, weren't around to hear. Pasting a smile on her face, Xandie corrected Zach's relative. "Agatha Braun explained to me that the ring was given to Zach's great, great, whatever grandfather, when he decided to leave Germany. As the eldest, the ring came to him."

Eric glared. "This is a lie. Our ancestors would not have done this. The ring was not his to gift, and we will be the Brauns to restore our shifter greatness and honor."

"By whatever means necessary." Sofie's wide grin turned feral.

Slapping the table with a hand that featured the disputed heirloom, Xandie raised her voice. "Is that a threat?"

"I have no clue what you mean. Must be my poor grasp of the English language." Sofie stepped forward, and her plate tipped. The pasta slid off and landed all over Xandie's hand and the heirloom ring. "I have such a poor grasp of everything, it seems." Sofie dumped her plate on the table and linked arms with her equally hulking brother. "You should get the ring cleaned. We'd hate to take our heirloom home stinking of American food products."

"Why, that..." Xandie grabbed a handful of the pasta and pitched it at the back of the female bear shifter's head. She smirked as a squeal echoed through a momentary karaoke lull.

Spinning, Sofie lurched to a table and grabbed a handful of bread rolls, firing the dough off like live grenades at Xandie.

Leaping to her feet, Xandie danced to the side, ducking and weaving until she came up against the karaoke stage.

"And I thought Elspeth would be the one to end the night in carnage. After all these years, I can still be surprised. Delightful discovery." Theo, Xandie's black feline guardian to the Supernatural Great Library of Alexandria, picked a strand of pasta off the front of her sparkly cream shirt. "Look, you blend with your food. I call that a solid win."

Ignoring her feline's sarcastic comments, Xandie straightened and dusted off her hands. "Is that all you've got? I feel let down. Harrows would never look so weak in public."

"Argh." Screaming, Sofie picked up a bottle of Witchshine and shook it furiously before aiming it at

Xandie and Theo. Ignoring the combined screams of horror from the other Harrows, Sofie let loose the cork. An iridescent stream exploded from the bottle, the force powerful enough to knock the shifter to the ground.

The blast of Witchshine spread out, covering the floor, stage, Xandie, and Theo, even knocking the stage props down and leveling the entire area.

"Not the fur. Please, not the fur. It will take me ages to get that Harrow brewed mess out," Theo wailed, laying spread-eagle across the stage floor.

The back yard erupted into mayhem as declarations of war were screeched from both families. Food flew, coming in hot from all directions.

Sofie crouched on the dance floor, eyes wide, mouth open in shock.

"I'm coming, doll face. No one disses my girls but me." Colin, Elspeth's enchanted, belching pug with chronic stomach issues, wobbled up to the bear shifter as fast as his puggish legs could carry him.

"You aren't welcome here, shifter. Take this as your eviction notice." He spun around, and wiggled, sighing in relief as a green cloud of seafood-scented fog covered the dance floor and the German bear shifter.

"Colin, no,." Xandie screeched the warning just a moment too late. She pulled her shirt over her eyes and attempted to crawl away. Until she met a pair of black and silver velour-covered legs with matching sneakers.

"If you didn't like karaoke, all you had to do was tell me."

Xandie stared up into the twinkling amber eyes of her wicked witch grandmother.

"Can I throw a party or what?"

THREE

"You can't blame this on Elspeth for once."

Xandie glared daggers at Holly. "I can blame whomever I want. And for now, it's Elspeth for planning a party and that one-eyebrowed Sofie Braun. None of this is my fault." Xandie pushed the door open and stepped into the shadow-filled jeweler's store.

Last night's food fight/karaoke engagement party had ended with a putrid bang. Colin, the pug, had effectively cleared the guests out. Even Zach's German relatives had left at a fast trot, still busily decrying Xandie's right to hold their precious heirloom ring. She held out the now begrimed heirloom. The silver band had faint markings around the edge, but age had worn off the details. A single pear-shaped amber stone sat in the center. The same stone that felt disturbingly sticky and loose in its setting.

"Elegant piece. Are you here to sell it?" A deep rough voice surprised Xandie, and she squeaked, dropping her hand.

Holly rolled her eyes. "Her fiancé's family would collectively throttle her."

Clearing her throat, Xandie twisted off the ring and held it out. "We had a food incident at a family party last night. I wonder if you could clean the ring?"

The jeweler stepped out of a shadowy corner and clucked his tongue as he took the ring and examined it. His eyebrows rose. "I did hear about the karaoke party at Harrow House last night. Wasn't it raided by the local police?"

"Point Muse gossip." Xandie twitched a polite smile at the wizened man. Elspeth would have towered over the jeweler in her stockinged five feet. She watched as he stroked his neatly trimmed gray beard. "My fiancé is the police chief in Point Muse. It was an overprotective pug with stomach issues that broke the party up."

"Yes. Yes. Of course." The jeweler waved Xandie's comments away. He lifted his head and fixed dark brown, beady eyes on the Librarian. "This is a very old piece of jewelry. The stone was added quite a bit later and is some-what loose."

Xandie winced. "That may have been caused by flying bread roll grenades."

The jeweler's eyes widened. "Antique pieces like this must be protected. I'll clean the ring and fix the loose stone." The little man drew out a velvet cloth and carefully laid the ring on it. "Ernest Gem is my name, and this is my store. Gem and Sons."

"Family store. That's cool," Holly piped up. "Our family business is mayhem."

"Elspeth Harrow." Ernest shuddered. "I avoid her. I prefer a more sedate life, and the sons of my sign were wishful thinking. I am currently unattached." He grimaced. "Dwarf women are flighty. They don't like to settle down much before they turn one hundred." He shuffled over to a counter and reached behind to pull out a bright red book which he slipped on the counter. "Now, name and details, please." He opened the book to a blank page and waggled bushy gray eyebrows at the women.

"Alexandra Meyers, engagement ring damaged by a family food fight." Xandie picked the ring up from the cloth and poked the stone. Yep, definitely loose.

Ernest scribbled in the book for a moment, then slammed it shut. He extended his hand, beady eyes glittering. "Your ring, please." He bared his yellow teeth in an encouraging smile. "I'll look after it as if it were my own."

Xandie's heart sped up. Why did she suddenly have the urge to hide the ring away from the dwarf?

Holly frowned and nudged her cousin. "Hurry up and give him the ring. We still have to make the meeting for the funfair."

Reluctantly, Xandie held out the heirloom and opened her fingers, so the ring lay flat on her palm. "Sorry. The ring belongs to my fiancé's family. I want to make sure it's safe."

The jeweler's hand closed over the ring, then he jerked it away from Xandie. "I have a backlog of orders to get through before I can repair the ring today. I will notify you when it's ready to be picked up. It shouldn't be too long." He shuffled forward and made a shooing motion with his hands as he herded the women toward the exit.

"Ah, any idea how long it will take?" Xandie asked over her shoulder as the dwarf shoved them out the door.

"As long as it takes. In the end, it's all about the quality. Thank you for your business." Ernest slammed the door shut behind the women, locking it and slapping a closed sign on the window.

"Is it my imagination or are the residents of Point Muse getting stranger?"

Holly shrugged. "Nothing surprises me anymore about this town. But he did seem overly eager to get us out of the shop."

Xandie glanced along Point Muse's cobbled Main Street. Point Muse lay on a nexus of ley lines and attracted supernaturals from all over the world to the coastal marine town. A mixture of stone and wood buildings with pretty gables, cobbled roads, and wrought iron lamp posts gave the town an old-fashioned vintage atmosphere. "I've got a bad feeling, and you know what happens then..."

"Someone ends up dead and I have to go to work?"

Her cousin, a banshee witch hybrid, worked at the Elysian Fields Funeral Home, owned by creepy twin necromancers, Hector and Hillary. And unfortunately, over the last few years, the funeral home had seen more than one victim of foul play in Point Muse. "At least you're keeping busy and away from Elspeth."

"True. Living in Harrow house with the wicked witch of Point Muse and my mother isn't one of my lifetime goals." Holly sidestepped a miniature ex-racing unicorn as it passed along the pavement next to its owner. "Oi. Watch it, Harriet. Don't make me turn you into the police for horn violations," Holly yelled at the tiny unicorn as it gestured rudely with its horn.

"What is with you and that mini corn?"

"It's a nasty piece of work. All mini corns are. I think they have compensating-for-their-size issues."

Harrows were crazy. Thankfully, Xandie was a Meyers. She paused at the entrance to Point Muse Park. "I'm so glad the town removed the statue of Elspeth as mayor. Kids kept putting wigs and underwear on it. It discombobulated me."

"Actually, I think that was Elspeth. She likes to be the center of attention." Holly pointed to a group of people marching toward them. "Gird your Librarian loins. We're about to be mobbed." She prudently stepped behind her cousin.

Bracing herself for the Point Muse fair committee, Xandie tried to look enthusiastic. Being the Librarian to the Supernatural Great Library of Alexandria was a big responsibility and unfortunately that meant she was the go-to for volunteering for any community activity in town.

"Alexandra Meyers. It is such a pleasure to meet you. Your Aunt Winifred has told us so much about you." A tall woman, with bright green eyes and long blonde hair, rushed up and shook Xandie's hand. "It's such an honor to meet the famous Librarian."

"Not that famous." Xandie slipped her hand out of the woman's tight grip and wiped it on her jeans.

"The cachet *the* Library brings to Point Muse and by extension, to our little fair, shouldn't be ignored. Family honor must always be upheld and respected." The woman's smile soured for a moment before returning at full blast. "How silly I am. I haven't introduced myself. Sabine Germani, event organizer. At your service." She gave a little bob up and down.

"Well, you know me. But this is my cousin, Holly, Winifred's daughter."

"The undertaker." Sabine inclined her head like a queen granting an audience to one not worthy of her attention.

"Banshee, and a Harrow, who just happens to work in a funeral home," Xandie corrected the overly snooty woman.

Winifred rushed up and muscled between her niece and the event organizer. "Thank you for doing the introductions, Sabine." She snagged Xandie and Holly's arms and hauled them over to the other two people waiting to the side. "And, of course, you know Horace." Winifred beamed at a short, broad, older gentleman. "He's kindly helping on the funfair committee, along with Milly Rosa."

"Mr. Painter. Fancy seeing you again."

Horace smoothed his gray hair and cleared his throat. "Librarian. Good to see you helping at the fair."

"Uh-huh." Xandie eyed the older man up and down. Last time she saw the gray-haired skirt chaser he'd been sipping from a hip flask, vowing revenge on the pastor as a food fight raged around him.

"You're wondering why Horace is here, aren't you?" A tall, angular, lavender-haired woman next to Horace patted his chest affectionately. "My Horace has turned over a new leaf. No more hip flask, and he's taking anger management classes daily. He is very Zen now. We even garden together." The older woman held out a hand. "Milly Rosa. Organizer of this group. I came to town just before the church incident."

"Before the church groupie lost it and went on a rival killing spree?" Holly glared as her mother pinched her arm. "It's true."

"We don't mention it though. We're here to support the funding committee and the Point Muse fair."

"And I do have other things to do today, no offense, Librarian," Sabine cut in and tapped her clipboard. "We're due to open shortly, and everything must be perfect."

"Of course, Sabine. Let me give Xandie and Holly the tour and outline their roles." Winifred clapped her hands, a twinkle in her amber eyes. "It'll be a family outing."

"Fine. It's your time, Winifred." Sabine snapped a sharp nod at Xandie and strode off, military precision to her movements.

Horace let out a gusty breath. "That woman and her clipboard scare me."

"Oh, sweetie. It's a confidence issue for the poor girl. You just stick to your own search for inner peace." Milly winked at her beau. "Why don't you head off and see if the sideshows have everything they need. I'll help Winnie with the tour."

Shooting Xandie and Holly a self-conscious glance, he leaned over and bussed Milly on the cheek before shuffling off.

"He's such a sweet man."

"I don't think Elspeth would agree." Mind you, Xandie's grandmother didn't much like anyone except for her noxious pug.

Winifred tapped her foot. "Let's get this tour on the go. Sabine will be timing us, and no one wants to cross her." Xandie's aunt led the way into the fair. She gestured to the left. "That way is sideshow alley. Ring toss, sharpshooting, dunk tank, that sort of thing. Then we have a carousel, spinning teacups, pony rides, and the tilt-a-whirl." Winifred frowned. "Don't let Elspeth go near the tilt-a-whirl. She's addicted to it, and no one needs a brain-addled wicked witch on their hands." She pulled up in front of a large tent and flapped a hand in its direction. "This houses our jugglers, clowns, displays, and small shows. It's our main exhibition area." Winifred held the flap open and ushered the others in.

"I love watching clowns. Some people find them off-putting, but I just adore them." Milly beamed as brightly dressed clowns tumbled past.

"Heads up," a cheerful voice bellowed as a juggling pin flew overhead. A tiny, curly haired, blonde woman, dressed in a blue doll outfit, cartwheeled past to grab the errant juggling pin. She turned flips until she landed back in front of the group. "Soz. Sometimes the pins have a mind of their own." She winked at the women. "Welcome to our fair. I'm Charlie Locks, juggler and gopher extraordinaire." She dropped a little curtsy and stared expectantly at Winifred.

Jolting, Winifred blushed at her lack of introduction. "Charlie is a jack of all trades but was hired for her juggling and tumbling."

Xandie held out her hand. "Hi. I'm Xandie Meyers. And this is my cousin, Holly."

Charlie widened her cornflower blue eyes. "Banshee *and* the Librarian. I've heard a lot about you both. Harrows are famous."

"Infamous you mean," Holly muttered, then winced as her mother elbowed her.

"Miranda can't stop talking about her family while she practices her knife throwing. It's so sweet." Charlie beamed, her blonde Shirley Temple curls bobbing as she shifted from foot to foot.

Miranda Harrow had never been called sweet in her life. Dangerous maybe, sweet, never. But her mother did like to play with knives. Xandie turned around. "Is anyone else from town taking part in the fair?"

"Elspeth's managing the dunk tank. Lila and the Devlin's are catering. I'm management, and Holly's kindly agreed to man the fortune teller tent since our regular lady quit a few days ago."

And in that whole sentence, Xandie was never mentioned. "And me? What do you want me to do?"

Winifred beamed at her niece. "You're our gopher. I'll explain later."

"That doesn't sound very appetizing," Xandie grumbled.

"It means you're a go-getter. You go get this, girl. Get that." Charlie giggled and flicked back into a handstand.

"Fantastic." Perky people headed her top pet peeves list.

"It's not as bad as it sounds. Some people can't leave their stalls, so the gopher helps." Milly wound an arm around Xandie's waist and dragged her to a tall, slim man with long blond hair in a braid, who stood behind a table filled with glittering jewelry. "This is Simon Wald. He's our jewelry artist. His pieces are divine."

"Yes, they are. And expensive too." He stared down his aquiline nose at Xandie, bright blue eyes glinting. "I have a talent for matching jewelry to people and their needs. But I reserve the right to refuse a sale if I don't think my jewelry will find a match."

Wow, the man obviously had a high impression of himself and his skills. Xandie looked over his stall. It was lined with silver of all shapes and sizes, covered in colorful gems.. Elaborate hair pins, brooches, rings, bracelets, earrings, and even engraved hair combs were all on offer.

"Anything take your fancy?"

Xandie shook her head. "I'm not really a jewelry person."

Simon sniffed. "Shame. With fingers like that, you could show a ring to perfection."

"Let's not talk about rings. It's a sore spot." Xandie formed a smile. "Everything is beautiful. I'm sure Point Muse residents will be lined up to buy stuff."

"Stuff." Simon raised an eyebrow before nodding a dismissive goodbye to the group of women.

Milly dragged Xandie to the exit. "Sorry. I should have warned you. Simon is a tad stuffy; it must be the English in him."

Stuffy wasn't the word Xandie would have used. "He's English?"

"Spent years living there, learning his trade. It's a family business apparently."

"There you are." Winifred frowned. "You have to keep up. Sabine won't be impressed if we fall behind schedule."

Holly rolled her eyes behind her mother's back.

"Don't think I don't know what you're doing behind me, Holly Harrow. I'm a mother. I have eyes in the back of my head, remember?"

Ignoring the bickering, Xandie glanced around the park. The town council in their infinite wisdom had decided to plan a large green space near the docks, so people could rest and relax and enjoy the town's attractions. They'd decided the small fair would be perfectly placed in the park. Xandie didn't know about rest and relaxation, but the briny smell of the ocean reminded her it was time for lunch.

Something fluttered out of the corner of Xandie's sight, grabbing her attention. Squinting, she spotted a familiar back disappearing around the corner. Why would her supposedly very busy jeweler be taking a side trip to a fair that wasn't even open yet?"

FOUR

"He said it wouldn't take long." Xandie tapped her fingers on Lila's table.

"He also said he had a backlog. It's only been twenty-four hours. Give him a break." Lila dumped a plate of green iced cakes in front of Xandie. "Try these, they might help."

"What are they?" Xandie grabbed a cake and munched, fighting the urge to roll her eyes back in her head. Her cousin really did have a talent for baking. Muted warmth spread through Xandie's midsection, and she released a breath.

"Coconut and lime calm-down mini cupcakes. I figured you needed a boost."

Xandie smiled gratefully. "Thanks." Lila was the drama llama of the family, but she knew her way around the kitchen and had a knack for helping calm people's issues with sugar. Lila's bakery, Hearts Delight, was her pride and joy. It had a hand-painted sign out front, along with a small, ornate white table and chairs. Inside the store, a fireplace dominated the room. A real, old-fashioned, stone hearth that in winter would pump out heat. Sitting resplendent opposite the fire was a blue velvet sofa. White painted wooden tables and comfy chairs dotted the room along with multiple glass cabinets filled with witchy pastries of goodness. Speaking of sugary treats, Xandie grabbed another cake. "Are you serving these at the fair?"

Lila nodded. "Ruby and Rose Devlin are bringing chocolates and small, decadent desserts and some savories. I'm focusing on cakes, slices, and finger food. It's a good combination."

"Uh-huh," Xandie granted. She still didn't trust those devilish Devlin twins one little bit.

"Suck it up, jealous Librarian. Braun put a ring on it. You win."

Xandie wiggled her fingers. "No ring on these babies right now. But that jeweler at the fair told me my fingers would show a ring off to perfection."

Lila snorted. "La di da. Aren't you lucky you have access to an old family heirloom?"

"Yeah. Lucky me." Xandie rested her head on her hands and stared morosely out the window onto Main Street. Truth be told, once the glow of the proposal had worn off and the ring sat on her finger, she'd finally had a good look at the Braun family heirloom. A wide silver band with flowers etched around the outside and a large amber stone. The stone stuck up loud and proud in the center of the ring. "The worst possible kind of ring for a Librarian who shelves books regularly," Xandie muttered to herself. She was terrified of bumping the ring whenever she shelved a book or a scroll and losing the stone. But then she felt guilty for not loving it. Harrow contrariness was a curse.

"Just tell him you don't like it, and he'll give it to his German cousins, and the family feud is over."

Xandie poked out her tongue at her meddling cousin.

"Two problems. He gave me the family ring to show I was part of his family, and I refuse to give into that food-throwing furry harpy, Sofie Braun." Xandie slumped into her chair. "I think I need another pick-me-up cake."

Lila snatched the baked goods out of Xandie's hand. "Stand down from the food coma, Sugarella. Just talk to Zach. He'll understand."

Slapping the table, Xandie stood and glared around the empty bakery. "I'm the Librarian. I've faced killer knights, demons, sulky sirens, and all manner of talking animals. I can do this."

"You're actually going to talk to Zach about the ring?" Lila shook her head. "My cakes work better than I thought."

"What?" Xandie looked horrified. "I'm going to storm Ernest and Sons jewelry store and demand my ring back. Food-fight stickiness or not." Xandie nodded and stormed straight toward the door.

"That's not quite what I had in mind." Lila stared at her determined cousin as she stomped away.

Marching along Main Street, Xandie psyched herself up. "You can do this. You're the Librarian. You're a tough, mouthy Harrow broad. You've got this." Reaching the door to Ernest & Sons jewelry store, Xandie tried the handle, but it refused to budge. "Typical," Xandie growled and flattened her face against the front window, peering in.

She could just make out the shapes of display cases and the old-fashioned till, but otherwise the interior was one gloomy mixed-up mess of shapes. Except for the one shadow that darted from the counter to the back doorway. Xandie thumped on the window and bellowed, "I can see you, Ernest. We need to talk. Are you listening to me? You'd better give my ring back, or you'll regret it. Violently."

"Everyone's listening to you and marveling at the fact your police chief fiancé isn't deaf already."

Xandie slowly turned, coming face-to-face with the German Braun matriarch, Mathilde Braun. Grandmother to Eric and Sofie Braun, the tiny bear matriarch measured in at below five feet. But her lack of height was made up for by her steel-straight spine and poisonous glare. "Mathilde, I see you're taking in the sights of Point Muse. Hopefully, everyone's been welcoming?"

"I've seen a sight that is a disappointment to the Braun name. To see a future relation caterwauling in the streets is a blow to the family honor."

First salvo fired. Xandie straightened and gritted her teeth before allowing herself a measured response. "Just making sure the jeweler fixes the ring quickly. My finger feels bare. That's all."

Mathilde's light blue eyes narrowed, and she thumped the ground with her heavy wooden walking stick and glared.

Even the old woman's no-nonsense gray hair, scraped back into a tight bun, was too scared to step out of place. Not to mention that cane with a large carved bear claw on top that looked as intimidating as Mathilde's matching brown skirt and top with sensible orthopedic shoes.

"The ring must be treated with respect. That is why it must travel back to the Black Forest and restore the family fortunes."

"That ring's been passed down through Zach's side of the family for generations."

"His side stole the ring before they deserted the rest of the family. It rightly belongs to the Black Forest Brauns." Mathilde's eyes blazed like blue fire. "We will not stand for this disrespect. We will have that ring, Librarian. No matter the cost. We will pay our debt."

"I can see everyone's getting along famously. Aren't they?" Xandie's Aunt Winifred popped up sporting a strained smile and forced herself in between the combatants. She grabbed her niece's elbow. "Sorry to interrupt, but Xandie's due at the fair opening this afternoon. We must be getting on." Winifred dragged Xandie down Main Street toward the fair. "Don't annoy the foreign side of Zach's family. They're cuckoo clock makers."

"And that makes them dangerous to annoy?"

"They're from the Black Forest. Who knows what kind of cuckoo clock curses they have access to?"

"I'm pretty sure Goldi Locks is the only person they've tried to curse through the ages." Apparently, Zach's great, great, however many greats, had a run-in with the golden-haired porridge thief. The Braun family came off second-best and had nursed a vendetta ever since. Much like the one Mathilde had for Xandie right now.

"Don't test them." Winifred gave a wave to the ticket seller as they passed the ticket booth. The funfair committee was right. The large grassy area near the marina was perfect for the community fund raising project.

"If it isn't the missing in action Librarian." Sabine smiled sweetly and tapped her ever present clipboard. "You must not have viewed the memo stating that all fair employees need to be present thirty minutes before opening for a staff meeting."

Whoops. Another person upset at her. "Sorry. Must've missed it. But I'm here now. What can I do to help?" Anything to take her mind off the Brauns' obsession with her engagement ring.

Sabine sniffed. Her green eyes narrowed as she considered the Librarian. She shoved a piece of paper at Xandie. "This is the list of our stallholders and sideshow operators. Work down the list, ask if they need anything. I'll dock your dinner break if I see you slacking." The event organizer snapped her heels like a soldier coming to attention and marched off.

"From suck-up to disdain within twenty-four hours. That must be a record."

"She just wants this to be a success. We *are* fund raising for charity, you know," Winifred soothed, then gave her niece a little pat on the back. "Hop to it, sweetie. Sabine wasn't kidding about docking your dinner break."

Blowing out a breath, Xandie scanned her list. "First up, the main tent and supercilious Simon, the silver jewelry maker."

"Have fun, dear." Winifred waved Xandie off.

Fun at a fair. She had a feeling that wasn't in the cards this afternoon.

"The great Librarian who doesn't wear jewelry. We are honored by your presence," Simon sardonically intoned as he shoved a piece of jewelry at a customer.

"Don't blame me for my ringless state. Blame my jeweler."

"Excuse me?" Simon turned away from his customer to stare at Xandie.

"I had to take my ring to the jeweler here in Point Muse. I'm currently chasing him to get an update on it. He seems to be avoiding me. And"—Xandie shook her paper—"I have a list of people to visit. Is there anything I can get you?"

"Yes. Yes, there is." Simon pointed to a coil of silver wire on his table. "I need another bolt of that. It's on my worktable in my van. You will fetch."

Said the master to the servant. He really was taking this

English overlord business to the extreme. She forced a smile. "Of course. And your van is where?"

"I can take you." Charlie, the golden-haired perky juggler, popped up next to Xandie.

Following at a more sedate pace, Xandie blinked as she stepped outside into the late afternoon sun.

"You get used to it."

"What?"

"In and out of the tent all day. Dim light to sunny. Gloomy to cheerful. That sort of thing."

"If you find the fair gloomy, why do you work here?" Charlie might find the fair gloomy, but the juggler certainly didn't look it. Her curly golden hair stood straight up, gelled into a purple-tipped mohawk which she matched with a lavender and pink clown outfit.

"I like moving around. Can't keep still. Working at fairs and circuses fits me." Charlie beamed a white toothy smile at Xandie and then pointed to a plain undecorated van that stood by itself at the edge of the fair. "That's Simon's. He prefers not to be too close to the hoi polloi of the fair." She flung the door open. "What does he need?"

Curious, Xandie took a step up into the van. "Silver wire coil." The van looked way bigger inside than she'd expected. One end held a bed and small kitchenette. The other housed a workbench full of metal parts grouped together in tidy piles. Paperwork with different drawn designs papered the floor under the bench.

"Not as tidy as I would've expected for a stiff upper lip Englishman." Charlie trailed fingers over the loose bits of metal and colored stones that covered the work area.

"I thought his accent sounded English." Stiff upper lip was right. He and Sabine would be a good match; both had equal disdain for the common people.

"Spent his schooling years in an English boarding school apparently. Probably accounts for his attitude." Charlie shifted forward and peered at the tiny kitchen before sticking her nose into a minuscule alcove that held Simon's bed.

"Aren't we supposed to be looking for wire?"

Spinning with a wide smile on her face, Charlie rummaged through her pocket until she held a coil of wire up victoriously. "Already ahead of you. I saw it when we first entered. I just wanted to have a quick peek around snooty Simon's van."

And just when had the juggler pocketed that wire? Xandie had eyes on her the whole time. Little perky Charlie had some suspiciously dodgy gifts. Xandie took a step forward and plucked the wire out of the juggler's hand. "Let's get this back to Simon before he has an elegant meltdown."

Charlie strolled back outside. "Normally, I can't stand a goody two-shoes, but on you, Librarian, it's a good look." She pointed to Xandie's list. "I can drop off English boy's wire if you want to catch up on your list. Sabine holds a grudge if her schedules are out of whack."

Biting her lip, Xandie looked from the wire in one hand to the list in the other. She wasn't completely sure she trusted the quick-fingered blonde, but Sabine was a scarier option. Decision made, she held out the wire. "Thanks, Charlie. I appreciate it."

Winking, Charlie snatched the wire from Xandie and skipped toward the main tent, hollering over a shoulder, "Now you owe me a favor, Librarian. And I never forget."

"Great. Ominous future favor hanging over my head. Something to look forward to." Xandie read over her list as she walked through the crowd of fairgoers. Not paying attention to her surroundings, she tripped over a tent peg. Pain ricocheted up her legs as she landed on her knees. The list ended up flat under her hand in a pile of mud. "Strike two for the Librarian." Sighing, she grimaced as she tried to wipe off the list.

"I told you not to talk to me in public."

A rough, grating voice Xandie recognized froze her cleaning efforts.

"You never answer your door. Where else am I supposed to talk to you?"

Why was Braun's cousin, Sofie, talking to Ernest Gem, her jeweler?

"That Librarian came around earlier, banging and yelling. I didn't have a choice."

"Well, you have a choice now," Sofie hissed. "You know what I want."

"A lot of people want it. Including that Harrow harridan. She threatened me. I don't respond well to threats. Now leave me alone. I'll contact you when I make up my mind."

The sound of Sofie's growl drove Xandie to her feet, and she scurried backward, away from the whispering conspirators. Sofie and Ernest were up to no good, and it was all Braun's family heirloom's fault. "How much worse can this day actually get?"

"My list."

Sabine's outraged tones grated along Xandie's spine. She'd spoken too soon. Xandie held up the grubby paper. "I slipped."

"And my paperwork broke your fall?" Sabine glared at the filthy, besmeared list.

"It's fine. I can still read it." Xandie attempted to shake off the worst of the mud without success.

A twitch flickered at the corner of Sabine's left eye. She pointed a trembling finger at Xandie. "Your dinner break is canceled. Consider this your one and only warning. Your family honor is at stake. Step up, Harrow." Sabine marched out of sight.

Xandie held up a hand. "Meyers, not Harrow." She winced as Sabine's high-pitched shriek floated back to her. All this talk about family honor and upholding the family name was getting repetitive. When it came to family, chaos and mayhem were locked into the Harrow gene pool.

This is all Elspeth's fault.

FIVE

"How many days left?"

"Too many days. The fair only opened yesterday at lunch." Holly shoved Xandie's feet off the chair and adjusted her turban. "Stinky feet do not go on seats."

Xandie groaned. "Is that a prediction?" She massaged the arch of her foot before slipping her shoes back on. "Besides, my feet hurt after all that running around Sabine had me doing last night. I didn't even get a dinner break because of the muddy list incident."

Holly whipped the cover off a crystal ball and hummed low in her throat as she considered its inner depths. "Madame Hollita sees it was your own fault you lost your dinner break. Next time, don't upset the woman in charge of your break time. So speaks Madame Hollita." Holly clapped her hands and smirked at her cousin. "What do you think?"

"That you're full of it. And it wasn't my fault I slipped."

"You were eavesdropping and probably weren't paying attention to where you were walking."

"You're dead to me. Do you hear me? Dead."

"Good thing I'm a banshee and can predict death."

"Not your own, remember? Speaking of death, I'm surprised your bosses let you do the fortune teller gig." Holly's bosses were twin necromancer descendants of Charon, the Ferryman of the Greek Underworld. And they took Goth to a whole new level.

"Business is slow at the funeral home, plus they want to support the community. So, they're okay with me working here when I can."

Xandie shuddered. "The less I think about your business, the better. The whole place creeps me out."

"You get used to it. It could be worse. At least this time we don't have a murderous dragon controlling the dead and recently buried."

"Good point." Watching Elspeth attack the walking dead in the cemetery would've been a horror lover's dream, but for Xandie, it was her worst nightmare.... That and hearing Elspeth scream Geronimo as she leaped on the zombies' backs.

"Here." Holly whipped off her bright orange and green turban and slapped it on Xandie's frizzy brown hair. "Make yourself useful. I need to have my dinner. I'll bring you something back from the catering tent."

"Gee, thanks. You're so kind." Xandie grimaced as she adjusted the turban. "Fine. Desert me. But you only have yourself to blame if people don't like my prophecies."

"Fortunes, love affairs, and happily ever after. Follow that formula and everyone's happy."

"Bet they don't have to contend with rabid foreign relatives wanting your family heirloom." With a weary groan, Xandie stood and stretched before standing in the small tent's doorway. She paused to watch fair goers ramble around. The fair had seen a pretty good turnout for the second day of trading. Looked like most of Point Muse had come out for an evening at the fair. Xandie spotted Sabine moving purposely toward her. She flipped the tent flap down in the hopes Sabine would think that Madame Hollita had a customer. Xandie twitched the flap open an inch and peered out. Sabine had veered off to have a heated conversation with a tall slim man with long, silver hair down to his waist. The fair organizer leaned toward the man with fisted hands on her hips. At the same time, her co-arguer took a step back. Throwing her hands up, Sabine stomped off down the sideshow alley, leaving her verbal sparring partner to blend back into the crowd.

"This place is a hotbed of passion.... And corn dogs. Lots of corn dogs." Colin, Elspeth's minion and talking pug, wobbled to Xandie and collapsed on her feet.

"Maybe you should slow the eating down. You might explode." She shook the dog off her feet and took a sidestep.

Colin let out an echoing burp and then rolled onto his back. "I'm in training, doll face. They've got a hotdog eating contest for the finale of the fair. My queen entered me as a secret weapon."

"Of course, she did. Anything to break the rules and win." And Colin was a shoo-in to win. A four-legged eating machine. "Hang on. I thought mom's knife throwing exhibition was the finale of the show?" Xandie's mother, Miranda, had worked as a black ops' agent for years. Expert knife throwing was a prerequisite.

"That's what they're saying, but it's really all about the food. You can at least count on the food not to stab you in the back." Colin rolled onto his feet and shook the grass off his coat.

"We can count on your scarfing down a trailer load of hot dogs."

"Just saying. The food here is the most normal bit about this entire fair." The pug padded around the fortune teller's tent. "You have people who smell like silver, those who smell like greed and death, and others who smell like grass and plants. This place is weird. Watch your back. I'm going for my third dinner. So long, kid."

Colin's eating habits were a long-established weapon of mass destruction that Elspeth wielded unwisely most of the time. Thankfully, he was on the Harrow side, although there'd been a few friendly fire incidents. Xandie flipped the tent flap up, ready for Madame Hollita's fortune telling to start. The crowd milled around the park, and Xandie waved to the faces she recognized from town.

A familiar figure with a curly, bouncy gold and neon pink ponytail weaved between the fairgoers. Charlie Locks was out on a perky rampage through the crowd, entertaining them with juggling and tumbling. Xandie watched the juggler caper around, pausing every so often to peek into a performance tent or stall. "Just what are you looking for, perky one?" Xandie mused.

Someone else grabbed Xandie's attention off to the side of the tents. This one was rough and unkempt as opposed to perky and over the top colorful. The man had a patchy, black beard and a ripped blue top that had seen better days. She tracked him as he made a beeline to the side of the main tent. Simon, the jewelry maker, pulled the man to the side and handed a small package off to him. In return, the man pushed a tattered envelope at Simon before disappearing around the side of the tent.

"Curiouser and curiouser." Just why had those two organized a clandestine meeting? Simon's mystery buyer didn't seem the type to go in for ornate silver jewelry. So, why all the cloak and dagger?

"Alexandra Meyers?"

A thin, weedy voice shocked Xandie from her musings. She adjusted her turban. "Madame Hollita is on break. But I, Xandeena, have a strong connection to the ether and can answer all your questions." Xandie dropped into a sweeping bow which lost impact when her turban dropped off onto the grass. "Whoops. Sorry. Please come in." She leaned down and quickly snatched the turban up before straightening.

"You are Alexandra Meyers? The Librarian to the Supernatural Great Library of Alexandria, are you not?"

"I am. You aren't here for a reading?" Turban in hand, Xandie stared at the tall man in front of her. The same man Sabine had a heated argument with earlier. Tall and slim with long silver hair and iridescent green eyes, the man made an impact. As did the gray, pinstriped Armani suit. Not normal attire for an appointment with a fortune teller.

The man sniffed. "I have no desire to hear lies and false-hoods about my fortune. I am on a mission of great importance for my mistress." He snapped a pristine white business card at Xandie.

Gingerly taking the card, Xandie read aloud, "Tyr Greenhand, secretary to Lady Rosalind Greenhand."

"I've been directed to negotiate with you, with regards to the family heirloom the bear shifters claim is theirs."

Why did it always come down to that ugly ring? "It isn't a claim. Their descendant was given the ring before my fiancé's side of the family immigrated to America."

"I think you'll find there is a viable dispute over the original ownership. It is of fae design and fae should control its power."

"Fae?" That's where the silver hair and glowing green eyes came in.

"Aos si, sidhe, fairy, fae. Humans have many names for my race. But my lady wants her property back. She has been patient throughout the years, but the Librarian should know better than to wear an oath-sworn ring. My mistress would not see such an august person as yourself make an error in judgment. Of course, there are other interested parties as well, but milady is prepared to be quite generous. She is actively looking to reacquire her ring." The fae looked down his nose at Xandie in her stained jeans, colorful shirt, and turban and sneered. "Although I cannot imagine why she would bother with one such as you."

So much for negotiating. Xandie held up the business card and deliberately ripped it in half. "That's what I think about your offer and attitude."

He gasped. *"The insult."* The fae reached for a slim sword buckled to his side that until now had remained invisible.

"That isn't a good idea, sir. I'd hate to have a fae-shifter incident." Zach Braun, police chief, bear, and Xandie's fiancé, stepped in front of his girlfriend and huffed, the sound low and rumbly, a warning for the other man to back off.

The fae's hand drifted away from his rapier. "This... This... human has done me the great disservice of destroying my calling card. This is an insult I will not forget."

"Hey." Xandie tried to shove past her fiancé, but he'd grown a bear hump on the top of his shoulders and blocked her way. She peered around. "You said my engagement ring wasn't a Braun heirloom, and you implied it'd been stolen. In my book, you insulted me first."

The fae drew himself into a stiff line of outrage. "I

implied nothing. Just stated the truth. You're a Librarian. Do your research."

Braun rumbled low in his throat again. "You need to move along, sir. This is a public area, and any disagreement should be conducted privately. Preferably with me, since it's my family's ring."

Narrowing his eyes until only a slit of emerald-green remained, the slim fae took a step back. "I see I have misjudged my timing. I am staying at the Mayweather Inn. We can conduct our negotiations in private there." With a regal nod, he picked this way through the crowd with a grimace playing over his face.

"Goodness. What a disagreeable man."

Milly Rosa, fair committee member, popped up next to Xandie. "Are you okay, dear?"

"That should be my line." Braun turned from watching the fae and pulled Xandie into a warm bear hug.

Sinking into his tight grip, Xandie smiled against his muscled chest. He always smelled like honey buns. Not surprising since all the Brauns in town had a crazed addiction to honey and Lila's baking. "I'm fine. But he wanted your ring. Just like everyone else in this town." Xandie pushed out of the circle of Zach's arms and flicked him between the eyes. "Time to pluck your monobrow again." Whenever her fiancé got anxious or protective over her, he grew a monobrow and a bear hump on his back. She'd only see him fully change a few times, but it was memorable... including the bare flesh afterward.

"I'd rather grow a monobrow than see you skewered by a fae rapier."

"He's aos si?" Milly smoothed her lavender-colored, chin length bob. "My goodness. Point Muse is full of surprises."

"You've heard of the fae?" Maybe the snooty man was right. Xandie needed to have a research session in the Library. She hated being unprepared.

"One hears a few things when you get to be my age. I'm sure you as the Librarian know more about them than I do."

"Not as much as you'd think."

"You need to head home and keep out of trouble. We'll work out what's going on as long as you're not spitted on a sword." Zach reached out a hand and tugged Xandie in for a gentle kiss.

Milly cleared her throat. "I can take over until Holly gets back if you want. That way you can head off early. In fact, I'm sure I heard your cousin, Lila, mention she was heading home soon too. You might be able to catch a ride."

"Safety in numbers from pointy things. I guess I should see if she's ready." Xandie handed the turban over to a helpful Milly. "Right, no need to worry. I'll head to the catering tent. Pick up Lila and head home. But"—Xandie pointed a finger at her fiancé—"We will speak about this ring later. Got it?"

Saluting, Braun brushed a kiss over Xandie's cheek. "I love it when you use your assertive Librarian voice." He winked and sauntered off into the crowd.

Xandie admired his tall, muscular frame. Solid muscles and wide shoulders, paired with a chiseled jaw, shaggy brownish hair, and piercing blue eyes, made for an attractive package, even with the odd monobrow issue.

"Off you go, dear." Milly shooed Xandie away.

Taking the hint, Xandie headed for the catering tent. As it happened, Lila stood outside it, stretching, when Xandie trudged up.

"Aren't you supposed to be the great Hollita right now?"

"Minor incident with a fae and a sword."

"What?"

Xandie held up a hand to stop the questions tumbling off Lila's tongue. "I'll explain on the way home, but first we need to take a detour."

Lila shut her mouth and nodded. "Okay, where's the detour?"

"We are going to see a dwarf about an heirloom. I think there's more going on here than just a family feud." And she needed to shut the drama down before the body count started...

It's Point Muse after all.

SIX

"I can't believe you had Great-Aunt Rose's finger stashed away in your vehicular deathtrap." Lila's work van was a rattletrap, but when she catered, a four-wheeled vehicle was a necessity. Most of the Harrows didn't drive, with the exception of Elspeth and Holly's mopeds and Lila's van. For some reason, the rest of the clans' skills did not extend to mayhem free driving.

"Correction. I had a copy of Elspeth's skeleton key in my van. Not the actual key."

Xandie shuddered. "It still creeps me out that the original skeleton key is a relative's finger."

"Welcome to the freaky world of the Harrow clan." Lila grunted and shoved the back door to the jeweler's store open. "Ta-da. Just as good as the original. Without the ick factor." Lila knelt next to a large, black hellhound and whispered, "Right, Nash. You're up. Scout the area and let us know if the coast is clear."

The hellhound's eyes flickered red for a moment before settling back into his normal chocolate brown. Nash had been a gift from Lila's father, Shade, head of security for

Hades, the God of the Underworld. Xandie winked at Lila's sidekick.

Nash let out a rumble. "Stay, pet." He slunk inside the darkened shop.

"How many times do I have to say it? You're the pet. Not *me*." Lila slumped against the wall of the jeweler's shop. "Runt of the litter, my sugared butter puffs. I think his mom, Cerberus, just couldn't stand his talking back anymore."

Ignoring her cousin's ramblings, Xandie waited for the hellhound's all clear signal, which came a few seconds later in the form of flickering red eyes.

"Safe." The low grated word slipped out from the shadowed jewelry store.

Xandie slipped inside, Lila at her heels. Something was definitely hinky with the Braun family heirloom. Too many people were interested in the tarnished ring *and* her jeweler had a secret meeting with the enemy. She needed to find out exactly what was going on.

"I forgot Elspeth's light balls. They would've come in handy." Lila cursed as she walked into a box.

"Shh. It'll be lighter in the front of the shop with a lamppost just outside."

"How do you know the ring isn't in the back room?"

"I don't, but considering how many people are after it, he'd probably want it close." Xandie squinted and carefully stepped around a small set of tables and chairs shoved against a mountain of boxes. "Besides, if it's in the back room, we're sunk. It's like a rabbit warren of cardboard boxes in here."

"And I thought *I* was messy."

Despite her denials, Lila thrived on chaos. Just like their grandmother. There was a reason the Harrows called Lila drama llama. "You *are* messy. But I get the feeling Ernest Gem has a few nefarious side dealings going on. Otherwise, why hide all these boxes out the back?"

"No room in his store or home?" Lila opened another metal door to expose a small room with bare shelves. "Okay. This guy is officially weird."

"Maybe he had a delivery tonight or a pickup first thing tomorrow?" Considering the amount of sneaking around good old Ernest Gem had done in the last few days, she had no doubt creepy midnight meetings were in the jeweler's regular schedule. Xandie eased the partially open door wider and stepped into the front of the shop.

Nash sat on the floor next to the door, panting quietly.

"Good boy." Xandie gave the hellhound a quick rub on his ears before starting the search for Braun's cursed ring. "See? I told you the lights outside would help."

Lila stepped out from behind a glass display case. "Congrats on being right. One little problem..."

"What?"

"All nocturnal activities are on display for most of Main Street. Including your police chief sweetie."

Xandie scuttled behind a counter that held an old-fashioned cash register. "Why didn't you tell me earlier?"

"What am I, the fun police?" Lila shrugged. "You had a plan you were proud of. I like to support a good non-Elspeth-related shenanigan."

Xandie crawled beside the counter, checking out shelves that held open and tipped over boxes. "Getting caught by my fiancé breaking and entering is kind of a wedding mood killer." She shoved a box out of the way, and its contents spilled across the floor. Cursing, Xandie tried to gather the contents back into the carton but gave up. The shop was a mess anyway. A large pile of open boxes lay in an uneven heap a few steps away. "It's a shambles back here. Looks like someone searched through every box looking for something."

"Your ring?"

"Maybe. The Hecate-cursed metal seems popular for some reason."

Nash growled low in his throat and paced in front of the back-room door.

"Make it quick, Librarian. The hound's getting restless."

"Then make sure we're all clear. The last thing we need is to be busted...again." Xandie crab-crawled forward, heading for the untidy heap of open boxes. Her ring might be in that pile since she hadn't seen it anywhere else. Xandie pushed a bundle of boxes to the side and squealed as she spotted her ring.

"I take it that's a good sign?"

"*Ha ha.* I knew that crafty jeweler couldn't hide my ring from me forever." She snatched the ring up and shoved it on her finger, wincing as something sharp bit into her knuckle. "So much for fixing the loose setting." Xandie made a face and shoved at the pile of boxes. Her eyes widened as the move uncovered what had been hidden underneath the disarray. "Why me?" Xandie groaned and scrambled away.

"Tell me you haven't found a talking rat and you're adopting it for your pet cat's pet imp?"

"Nope. Trust me. He won't be talking any time soon."

"Seriously? How many times do we have to break into a place and end up finding a body?"

Nash twitched and pawed at the back-room door.

"Cut it out, dog. You're in the doghouse. Why didn't you warn us about the body?" Lila grouched at her hellhound.

"Dead. Pet safe."

"Argh. I can't reason with you when you're like this." Lila threw up her hands. "How many times do I have to tell you? I feed you. You're the pet."

"Can we stop squabbling?" Xandie grabbed the corner of the counter and hauled herself to her feet. "We have to get out of here before someone finds us."

A click sounded in the still room before lights blazed overhead, illuminating the jewelry store, a pile of boxes, a lifeless arm, and Xandie and Lila frozen.

"Too late." The police chief sighed as he stepped into the front room. "I thought we talked about breaking and entering?"

Xandie pointed to Lila. "It's all her. She's a bad influence."

"Please." Lila rolled her eyes. "You're engaged. He knows exactly whose fault it is. Plus, it isn't breaking and entering if you have a key." Lila smirked and wiggled her skeleton key copy.

Braun grimaced. "Great-Aunt Rose?"

"A copy. Like Elspeth would let us borrow Rose's finger. Or let it slip through her greedy little hands," Lila snapped.

Braun held out his hand. "Key, please."

Lila slapped the key into the bear shifter's palm and glared at her cousin. "This is what I get for helping in one of your schemes. The fuzz has busted us and confiscated my illegally copied get-out-of-jail key from our Aunt Rose's finger. I blame you, cousin."

Xandie held her hands up in protest. "Hey. Don't hate the Librarian. Hate the person who offed my jeweler." She pointed at the partially uncovered body. "I knew he was up to no good. And somebody else agreed with me."

Braun pinched the bridge of his nose with one hand as he waved his twin brother deputies past. "Why is it that when we get an anonymous call about illegal activity, I always end up taking my fiancée back to the station?"

Xandie winked at her shifter. "Just lucky, I guess?"

"That's not the word I'd use." Braun pointed out back. "All of you, in the squad car. We are going to the station."

Wait until the German Brauns find out about the jeweler's body. Xandie would never hear the end of it.

"Let me get this straight." Zach tapped his fingers on the metal desk. "You saw Ernest Gem lurking around the fair, talking to people, and you decided you needed to break into his store."

"Plus, he had a secret meeting with cousin Sofie, and they weren't exactly complimentary about me and..." Xandie drew the word out. "He wouldn't give my ring back."

"This ring?" Braun pointed to the engagement ring that sat in the middle of the desk in an evidence bag.

Xandie rolled her eyes. "Yes, that ring. The same ring you gave me after you proposed. That ring."

"Why would Ernest Gem refuse to give it to you?"

"I don't know." Xandie slapped her hands on the table and glared at the police chief. "Why is everyone suddenly after it? Why aren't you questioning Sofie? Or that snooty fae staying at Mayweather Inn? I saw him fighting with Sabine. Actually, I saw Sabine grumping at him. But still, they were together." She sagged against her police issue folding chair. "I don't understand why people want it so bad anyway," she mumbled to herself.

"If you don't like it, you can pick something else. Obviously not from Ernest Gem's store though."

Xandie lifted her head at Zach's clipped tone. She jumped up and dodged the table before placing her cheek against his and giving him a bear hug. "I love the ring. It's just a bit bulky for shelving books and scrolls in the Library. I'm worried I'll lose the stone when I'm working and the setting was a bit loose. It needed a clean after the food fight as well. That's why I had Ernest look at it. That's all."

The stiffness flowed out of Braun. "Could the witness please stop giving the police chief a hug and sit back down? We can snuggle later."

Clearing her throat, Xandie slipped back into a chair and steepled her fingers. "Of course. Carry on, Police Chief Braun."

"After making the decision to search Gem and Sons jewelry store, did you see or hear anything suspicious?"

"Nothing." Xandie shook her head. "We sent Nash in to make sure everything was safe. A dead body is safe, so he didn't bother to tell us about him. Once we started searching, I kind of ran into Ernest and my ring." She poked at the evidence bag. "I don't think he's cleaned it. If anything, it looks worse. It has all this black gunk on it that's starting to flake off, and it kind of looks tarnished now. And the stone's still loose. So, he didn't repair it."

"Can we focus on the dead body?"

Smiling at her boyfriend, Xandie waved him on. "Of course, sweetie."

"Chief Braun when I'm interviewing you, please." Zach glared at Xandie. "Now, how did you recognize Mr. Gem if all the boxes were covering him?"

"By his stubby fingers grasping my ring. It was obvious." She leaned forward and narrowed her gaze. "How did he die? Death by ring boxes?"

Braun lowered his tone. "Since you're a witness, I

couldn't possibly tell you the results of the healer's inspection. But hypothetically, he could've died from the poisoned silver dragonfly hat pin shoved in his chest or the multiple ring boxes pushed down his throat. Hypothetically, of course." Zach raised his voice to normal tones. "Now, Ms. Meyers. Let's go over your whereabouts again."

"Seriously? You know I didn't kill him to get my ring back."

"Various people witnessed you banging on his shop door earlier and issuing threats against the deceased."

"If that's your mouthy cousin, Mathilde, you need to speak to her about her granddaughter's secret meetings with my jeweler." Xandie crossed her arms. Sofie and the jeweler hadn't exactly seemed like best buds when they had their meeting. But would Zach's cousin kill for the ring? Would Mathilde send Sofie on a mission to kill the jeweler and steal the ring? She couldn't see the old matriarch raising a finger to do it herself. Why did the two of them want it so bad?

"You can't go in there." The frantic tones of Zach's younger brother, Caleb, filtered through the door just before it slammed open, revealing Elspeth in her neon pink jogging suit glory.

"I need to retire." Zach rubbed his forehead.

"*You,*" Elspeth intoned in a fake deep voice, pointing an accusing finger at her soon-to-be grandson-in-law.

"Me. Lucky, lucky me." Braun closed his file. "I can see question time is done. What can I do for you, Elspeth?"

"Release my law-abiding granddaughter, you officious rule lover." Elspeth flung a pink braid over her shoulder and glared at the police chief through hot pink bangs.

Xandie shuddered. Cutesy didn't work for Elspeth. Her grandmother had a love bordering on obsession for wigs. No one, not even her own family, had seen her real hair in years. Add on her disdain for law enforcement and hurricane Elspeth had made landfall.

"She's my fiancée, and she isn't under arrest."

"Ain't no fuzz insulting my honorable family name with a trumped-up charge of murder."

"And breaking and entering," Zach added.

"They had a key. It's not breaking and entering if they have a key," Elspeth muttered under her breath. "Even if it was an illegally obtained copy they will pay for later." The wicked witch of Point Muse bounced on the balls of her feet, like a prizefighter warming up. "Now release the Librarian, copper. Or face the consequences." She wiggled her fuchsia painted nails, and blue arcs of electricity raced over her fingers, playing hide and seek.

Braun pushed his chair back from the table and waved Xandie off. "Feel free to take your grandmother and escape law enforcement clutches. Lila's waiting outside. Save my sanity and go as quickly as you can."

Jumping up, Xandie blew Zach a kiss as she joined Elspeth. "See you back at the Library, sweetie."

"Oh, right. That was easier than I thought it would be." Elspeth looked disappointed and dropped her hands. The electricity flickered out.

"It's okay, Elspeth. I'm sure you'll get to bust out your electric hands sometime soon." Xandie patted her grandmother's bony, pink velour-covered back before squeezing past her.

She needed to get to the Library and regroup. Someone killed her secretive jeweler, and Xandie had a feeling the Braun family ring was at the center of the trouble.

Just another day in Point Muse.

SEVEN

"It's the perky one. She's nosy, always hanging about asking questions." A stocky, bald man with a dirty shirt glared at the gathering crowd.

Perky. That could only mean Charlie Locks. Xandie leaned in next to Holly and whispered, "What's going on?"

Holly twitched her turban to the other side of her head. "Things have gone missing from some of the permanent fairgoers' vans. The bald one thinks it's that perky juggler. Looks like perkiness is a crime around here."

"Depends what time of the morning it is." Xandie fought the yawn that threatened to crack her jaw. After Elspeth had sprung her from the station, the Harrows had stayed up late, sharing arrest stories. A fair amount of chocolate and Witchshine had been consumed, and Xandie had opted to stay over instead of heading back to the Library like she'd planned. Waking to the chaotic Harrow household with a hangover made perky a curse word so she could understand the crowd's grumpiness.

"What is going on here? Why aren't you all at your stalls?" Sabine hurried over, her long blonde hair flying in a golden sheet behind her, clipboard clasped to her chest. "The fair is due to open, and you've all deserted your posts."

"Because of that juggler." The bald man pointed an accusing finger at Charlie.

"Me?" Charlie gasped and held a hand to her chest. Her straightened blonde and turquoise ponytail, matching her green and blue clown costume, swayed behind her back. "I am an open book. Ask me anything." She clapped her hands and skipped around in a circle, grinning madly.

"Did you steal my limited edition wicked witch of the year figurine?" Charlie's bald accuser growled.

Stopping her antics, Charlie stared, confused, at the man. "You're a grown man and you have a witch doll?"

The man's cheeks colored red. "Figurine and it's the wicked witch of the year. She's a limited edition, and this year comes with a pack of wigs and a small talking pug. Collector's item for sure. Now where is it?"

Hecate's cursed toenails. "Is he talking about Elspeth?"

"Colorful wig, check. Talking pug, check. A lifelong enjoyment of other people's suffering, check. Of course, it's her."

Xandie groaned at Holly's words. "We'll never live this down. Her ego will need a new zip code."

"Well? Where is my doll?"

"Figurine." Charlie shrugged, bemused. "I have no clue, but it wasn't me. I grew out of dolls years ago."

A bearded woman in a tight, corseted red dress shoved her way forward. "I saw you near the residential vans yesterday and today. And my gold-plated razor is missing."

"You're the bearded lady. Since when do you shave?" Charlie shot back.

"None of your business, blondie. But I want it back now."

A chorus of angry voices grew louder around Xandie. She'd seen Charlie slipping back into Simon's van the other day. The blonde juggler didn't really seem the type to steal a golden razor and a plastic doll though. But there was something furtive about the perky fair employee.

"Listen up." Sabine shook her clipboard at the furious crowd. "I'm sure Charlie won't mind us checking her van for any contraband. If there is any, she will be dealt with severely and, if not, this ruckus stops right now, and we all go back to work. Agreed?"

"I, too, have had some stock purloined. I will be interested to see if it appears in Ms. Locks' domicile." Simon, the silver maker, stood by himself off to the side.

"What did he say?" Holly looked over at Xandie.

"That's snooty talk for someone stole his jewelry and it might be in Charlie's van," Xandie translated. Simon Wald had a high opinion of himself, and his crisp English accent certainly helped foster that opinion. But he was just as suspicious as Charlie, with his secretive exchanges with that rough looking stranger.

"Right." Sabine nodded with a decisive jerk of her head. "Charlie, lead the way to the van. We can get this over and done with and get back to work."

Charlie skipped to the head of the angry mob and led them to her van. She unlocked the door and swung it open. "Mi casa es su casa. My house is your house. Search away." She leaned against the side of the hot pink van and beamed as Sabine gingerly entered the van.

Xandie pushed her way through the crowd. "You don't seem very worried about the search."

"If I were the thief, why would I store my ill-gotten goodies in my own van? Kind of stupid. Besides, I'm not a fan of dolls. Although the gold razor might come in handy." She snickered at her own words.

"That's true, but you did go into Simon's van," Xandie pointed out.

"As did you, if we're being fair."

"I meant a second time, by yourself. I saw you break into his van," Xandie prodded. Charlie might not be the fair thief, but she *was* up to something.

Charlie tapped her chin. "Is it breaking and entering? *Really?* I mean, if the doors are unlocked, you're entering but not really breaking."

Xandie rolled her eyes. "Seriously? Why does everyone argue about breaking and entering? Is your middle name Harrow?"

"Not that I know of, but my ancestors weren't exactly law-abiding. More like rule breakers. Who knows?"

"Right." Sabine stepped out of the van with two of the crowd who'd followed her in. "We've searched and found absolutely nothing in Ms. Locks' van. Can we please get back to work? The fair is open, and the customers are flowing in." Sabine slapped her clipboard, then glared at Xandie and Charlie. "No more scenes, Ms. Locks. I'm watching you." Sniffing, Sabine strode off toward the main tent.

"What?" Simon the silversmith, stood to the side of the crowd, fists clenched. "She's guilty. You're all blind."

Wow, someone had his hate on for the perky blonde. "Not defending her, but haven't you heard of innocent until proven guilty?"

"Her family's always guilty. It's the family business, thieving. I want my jewelry back." Simon crossed his arms and glared.

Charlie dropped her smirk. "I have nothing to do with my family or the missing items."

"She's hiding the items elsewhere. I know it.

Xandie pursed her lips. Why did Simon seem so sure about missing items being in Charlie's van? Maybe he'd hidden them there himself? But why would he want to incriminate Charlie? So many questions and not a lot of answers.

"Sorry to interrupt the finger-pointing, but we have a problem." Lila ran up next to Holly and leaned over, panting.

Munching on a pretzel from a small bag, Holly pointed at her cousin. "Isn't that tight-wound blonde with the clip-board in charge? Go whine to her."

"Shut it, banshee. We have a Harrow problem."

Xandie shook her head. "No. Not today. She promised. *She promised.*"

Lila straightened. "Well, she is the appointed wicked witch of the year. What did you expect?"

"*Elspeth.*" Xandie growled her grandmother's name through gritted teeth.

Was it too much to ask for peace while she tried to solve her greedy jeweler's murder?

"And your black forest cake is the worst I've ever eaten." Elspeth spotted her granddaughters and Charlie as they rushed up to the gathering crowd of onlookers. "Even my baker granddaughter's black forest cake is better than yours, you old hag."

"Hag?" Mathilde Braun shrieked and picked up a dirty,

gray ball from the pile in front of her. She lobbed it at the target on the side of the dunk tank.

"*Ha. Ha.* Obviously, Braun athletic acumen skipped a generation," Elspeth sneered and then conducted an inspection of her bright orange painted nails that matched her brightly colored, old-fashioned swim dress with bloomers underneath.

"You are a menace. You would not know a good black forest cake if it smacked you in your big mouth."

"For a bear shifter, your aim and strength are pitiful. Maybe you're a teddy bear shifter."

Mathilde shrieked a garbled comment back and grabbed two balls, launching them as hard as she could.

"Don't you think you should interfere?" Holly stepped behind Xandie.

"Why should I? Elspeth's manning the dunk tank. That's what's supposed to happen." Plus, Mathilde, even being below five feet, was just as scary as Elspeth. The old girl wielded that bear-claw-topped cane like a Kendo expert.

"It's your family. Think of it like Elspeth duty." Lila placed a hand on Xandie's back and shoved her hard enough she tumbled onto the grass next to Mathilde's pile of Elspeth bombs and the scary bear cane.

"*You.*" Mathilde took her attention off Elspeth for a few seconds to glare at Xandie. "This is all your doing."

"How is your feud with my grandmother my fault? I'm an innocent bystander in all of this."

Mathilde's German accent thickened. "You cheat the Braun clan out of their rightful inheritance. You with your conniving Librarian ways."

"This is all about the ring?"

"Yes," Mathilde bellowed. "Our family's curse. You steal it."

"Harrows are not thieves. Especially not our mayhem-free Librarian." Elspeth drew herself up on her perch. "How dare you insult the Harrow name."

"Meyers, soon-to-be Braun," Xandie offered weakly from her position on the ground.

"I don't care. I cry blood feud." Elspeth let out a high-pitched cackle. Thunder rumbled in the distance and the sky darkened.

"Maybe the simplest thing would be to hand over the ring and pick a new one. Family feuds are horrible to watch." Milly, tall, angular, with lavender hair, levered her hands under Xandie's armpits, hauling the Librarian to her feet.

"I don't have it anyway. The police do. It's evidence in Ernest Gem's murder." Xandie sighed. "Besides, how could I hand it back without upsetting my fiancé?"

Milly rubbed Xandie's back. "I'm sure you will work something out. You are the Librarian. That poor jeweler was murdered, I take it?"

"Poisoned hat pin through his chest and ring boxes shoved down his throat. Not exactly natural circumstances."

"My goodness." Milly clasped her hands together. "How frightening. And to think I only saw him at the fair the other day. Such a shock. Although..." She leaned in conspiratorially. "He wasn't exactly a nice man. Way too secretive and very grumpy."

Xandie smelled gossip in the air. "Really? What secrets?"

"Oh." Milly waved a hand airily. "Sadly, nothing specific, but I did see him meet with that snooty blond man a few times. And I wondered if that Braun girl was dating

Ernest as I saw them together too. You never can tell the dating habits of the young these days."

Braun girl? Melody Braun, Zach's younger sister, wouldn't be caught dead with the dwarf jeweler. So, who... "You mean Sofie?"

Milly nodded. "I saw them quite a few times. They mostly fought, which is why I thought they might be seeing each other. Fighting can be quite passionate, you know."

The meeting Xandie had spied on between Sofie and Ernest hadn't been the only one. Had Sofie been trying to buy the Braun family ring off the jeweler? Had she killed him when he refused? Xandie really needed to talk to the German girl. The smell of rubber burning tore Xandie away from her interrogation plan and back to the Harrow versus German Braun feud.

The pile of gray balls next to Mathilde now resembled a pile of gray goo. Mathilde shook the hand that gripped the last unmelted ball at Elspeth. "You think that will stop me, you black-hearted loose cannon?" She pulled her arm back and let the ball fly. It soared through the air until it hit the dunk tank target smack in the center.

Xandie closed her eyes and begged Hecate to swallow the dunk tank, saturated Elspeth, and the spiteful Mathilde whole. She warily opened her eyes. Sadly, the goddess had chosen not to answer. And now a bedraggled, sopping wet Elspeth glared with glowing amber eyes at the bear shifter matriarch.

The same old woman who currently engaged in a jubilant polka around the oozing pile of melted ball goo.

Some days aren't worth getting out of bed for.

EIGHT

"This is the seventh circle of hell, right? I'm here because I snapped and took out everyone. This is my punishment." Xandie played with her knife and fork and kept her eye on her dinner plate.

Zach rubbed Xandie's back. "None of us are dreaming, unfortunately. We are all living the insanity of a family dinner."

"Don't worry. I have my reaper scythe if the body count rises. I like to be prepared. I'll have to head out in the next few days, but I won't be gone long. Until then, you have my scythe at your beck and call." Matthew Grim, Point Muse's resident reaper and Lila's other half, poked his head around Xandie's fiancé and winked. "We're back-up if you need us."

"Bags not taking on Elspeth and Mathilde." Lila joined the conversation. "Those two are as nasty and evil as each other."

Holly poked Xandie in the ribs. "I second this. You and Zach get the evil grandmothers."

"Hey," Xandie protested. "That's not fair. I'm under

stress here. You should be lightening my load, not adding to it."

"We could let our mothers oversee them?" Holly shrugged.

Lila grimaced. "Your mother's probably packing a weapon anyway. But she might not be much help right now. She has a twitch thing going on at the moment."

The group stared at Miranda, Xandie's mom. As an ex-black ops' agent, she was normally the epitome of cool. But the strain of sitting between Elspeth and Mathilde at a family dinner at the Mayweather Inn was starting to tell. Her normally unruffled, gray-streaked, frizzy auburn hair was starting to stick up like she'd stuck a finger in an electrical outlet. On the other side of Elspeth sat Xandie's Aunt Winifred, who shot her elder sister a worried glance and tried to defuse the situation. "I'm sure Rose will be here any minute with our mains. Mayweather Inn always goes that extra mile for its guests. And how nice was it that Rose Mayweather gave us a private dining room for our *family* dinner?" Winifred stressed the family part of the sentence. Her plump cheeks glowed red as she fanned herself. "Is the air-conditioning off? It seems to be quite warm in here."

"Heated by the fires of my hatred." Elspeth glared at Mathilde. "I burn long and hard and don't you forget it."

"Except when you tangle with water, then..." Mathilde snapped her gnarled fingers. "You are nothing but a sopping wet, vanquished foe." She beamed at the table's occupants, her slightly crooked teeth glinting in the muted glow of the dining room. "I thought you witches would be heartier. Good strong shifter stock would never give in so easily." Mathilde's top lip curled as she considered Agatha Braun, Zach's mother, and Zach himself. "At least the Black Forest part of the clan wouldn't."

Sofie rolled her eyes. "It's their weaker blood. Our cousins have no staying power." She winked at Zach. "At least some of them don't."

Xandie growled and opened her mouth, but Holly's tiny foot mashed down on the top of hers, causing a pained grunt instead.

"Nothing weak about our bloodlines." A flash of red colored Zach's whiskery cheeks.

"Really? Why aren't your brothers or sister here?" Sofie smirked at Zach.

"I figured they were too scared to face the family dinner and ran away?" Eric, Sofie's elder brother, gnawed on a breadstick as he waited for the main course. His bushy eyebrows waggled as he chewed mechanically.

The bulky bear shifter's buzz cut couldn't quite hide the fact he had a monobrow issue. Thankfully, Zach's one eyebrow only popped up when he shifted. Normally, after running to Xandie's rescue in an Elspeth-related incident.

"My sons and daughter are on shift. Just because someone called a family dinner at the last minute doesn't mean crime stops here in Point Muse," Aggie growled at the younger bear.

Winifred's chin wobbled. "Sorry," she apologized quietly. "I called the family dinner tonight. I thought it would be a good idea to clear the air after the dunk tank incident earlier today."

"There was no incident. I, the superior supernatural creature, won. That is all."

Tapping filled the room. Elspeth clicked her orange painted nails against the tabletop. "That's not how I remember it, Mattie. I can call you Mattie since we're gonna be such a close family soon." The wicked witch of Point Muse bared her teeth in a predatory grimace.

"Your fragile mind remembers the event incorrectly. However, my strong bear genes tell me the truth." Mathilde wrinkled her nose. "Point Muse is as weak as its residents. And the lack of regular decency in this town can be linked directly back to those within power and law enforcement. I feel it is a problem these days."

"Why you..." Aggie Braun clenched her fist and started to move her chair when Winifred's hand clamped down tightly on her arm. Zach's mother subsided and glared at her plate.

"The lack of timely service in this town is also an issue," Mathilde continued her rant.

Rose Mayweather, owner of Mayweather Inn, resplendent in a pale lemon, fifties style house dress and sporting a silver bouffant hairdo, swept in with a handful of plates. Multiple servers followed the inn owner, laden with more plates of food. "Quality takes time, Mrs. Braun." She carefully placed a plate filled with rare steak in front of the elderly bear shifter.

"We shall see, Ms. Mayweather. We shall see."

Straightening, Rose stared at Xandie. "Alexandra, could I see you for a moment?" She cocked an eyebrow. "Outside, if we could." With a forced smile and a swish of petticoats, Rose sashayed out.

Xandie gazed longingly at her plate of fish and lobster tail tacos. Families were at war, especially on your appetite.

"It's okay. I don't have to fit into a wedding dress anytime soon, and it's a crime to let Rose's food get cold." Holly pushed her Caesar salad to the side and dragged Xandie's plate in front of her.

"You're so giving," Lila snarked.

The banshee grabbed a taco. "I try. I really do."

"The whole family is trying." Xandie stood and eyed

Zach's crabcakes. Part of being a couple was sharing every-thing, including crab cakes.

"We can share the crab when you come back." Zach offered a small smile. "By the way, the ring's been cleared as evidence. That's if you want it back." He held up the ring and quirked an eyebrow at Xandie. "Marry me...again?"

What could she say to that? "Of course, I will." Xandie grabbed the ring and slipped it onto her finger. She swore if she managed to track down the killer, she'd speak to Zach about changing his ring. She just needed to gather her courage first.

Zach grinned. "For a minute there, I thought you'd back out."

"Never." Xandie pointed at her fiancé. "You're stuck with me *and* the Harrows."

"Alexandra." Rose's annoyed tones rang out from the hallway.

Giving in, Xandie waved to her family before shuffling out of the room, dragging her feet. Rose Mayweather wasn't a card-carrying fan of the Harrow family, but she didn't want to start a feud with Elspeth. If she was pulling Xandie away from a meal she'd toiled over, something was up. Xandie closed the dining room door behind her and joined Rose in the middle of the hall opposite the bar. "What do you need, Rose?"

The hostess pursed her deep red, bee stung lips. "We aren't friends, Alexandra, and I abhor your family. But the Harrows perform a necessary evil in Point Muse."

Evil? The only evil she knew was her grandmother. "Keeping an eye on Elspeth?"

"Exactly." Rose nodded. "That and solving murders in Point Muse. Also because of the Library." She waved a hand in the air, dismissing Xandie's work.

"Uh-huh." Rose was definitely building to something.

"That's why I feel the need to tell you this for your own good. That stocky female bear, Sofie, has been sneaking around late at night. And last night, I heard her with a gentleman caller on the front porch."

Good old Sofie romancing a local? Xandie shuddered, pushing the image of the whiny bear shifter dating anyone out of her head. "What do you want me to do about it?"

"Well, dear, that's up to you. But if it were me, I wouldn't be impressed with my fiancé having a late-night rendezvous with other women. Even relatives."

A snort slipped out before Xandie could control it. "I don't think Zach is Sofie's midnight lover."

"Normally, I'd agree. He has somewhat better taste." Rose eyed Xandie's black jeans with a matching black top with *Librarians Shelve It Better* emblazoned in hot pink scrawled across her chest. "But she constantly talks about our police chief and that ring of yours." Rose peered at Xandie's finger. "It's somewhat concerning to myself as a business owner. And no offense but that's a truly horrid-looking engagement ring. I would have thought the Chief could manage something more non-tarnished."

Everything came back to that Hecate-cursed heirloom. Xandie forced a smile. "It was being repaired when the jeweler was killed. I'll get it looked at again. Once the murder is solved."

"Of course." Rose's forehead wrinkled. "Anyway, I thought you should just know what that Sofie is up to."

"You mean you just want to get a head start on the gossip." Elspeth suddenly appeared and stepped up to Rose in her pink combat boots that matched her dusty rose mohawk and neon pink jogging suit.

Rose took a prudent step back, hand to her heaving

bosom. "I would never gossip. I just think that Sofie woman is up to no good. And Alexandra should know."

"Job done. Now scoot. Stay out of the dining room for a while. Things are getting dicey in there." Elspeth cackled, and the chandelier overhead dimmed and shook for a moment before blazing bright.

Rose scuttled into the bar and slammed the door shut with a resounding bang.

Snickering, Elspeth held out a gray object to Xandie. "Here, I think you might need this tonight. Seems like a good time."

Gingerly unwrapping the unwanted gift, Xandie gagged as she caught sight of it and shoved it back at her grandmother. "Why did you give me that? You know Great-Aunt Rose's finger freaks me out."

Elspeth narrowed her eyes and pushed it back at her granddaughter. "Get over your wussiness. You need this more than I do. What better time than when everyone's busy sniping at each other in the dining room."

"What better time?" With Elspeth, she could mean anything. It was best to clarify.

"Search those wannabe bear shifters' rooms. Especially that mealy mouthed girl's."

Xandie pocketed her great-aunt's finger...just in case. "Why should I feel the need to search anyone's rooms?"

"Your jeweler is dead, and those Black Forest bears are after your ring. Something's up. Now scoot. I got me some distracting to do." Elspeth pushed her sleeves up, then cracked her knuckles.

"Toodles, granddaughter. Enjoy yourself. I know I will." She finger-waved to Xandie and marched back into the dining room.

Rose poked her head out of the bar doorway. "Rooms ten, eleven, and fourteen. If you're interested."

Xandie raised an eyebrow at Rose's eavesdropping.

Rose pointed upstairs. "They need watching. For once, Elspeth and I agree. Crack on, Librarian. I can only hold off dessert for so long."

Sighing, Xandie trudged up the staircase to the second level. "Talk about déjà vu." Xandie drew Great-Aunt Rose's skeleton key finger out and unlocked the door to room ten. "I'm searching other people's rooms so often I should be Xandie *'breaking and entering'* Meyers." She pushed the door open and stepped in, carefully closing it behind her. "Has to be Cousin Eric's room." Sofie's brother was a pig. A bearish, messy pig.

She grimaced as she stepped around a pile of dirty boxers left sitting in the middle of the floor. His bed lay unmade, suitcase open, and clothing strewn everywhere. Plates of half-eaten food covered the small table in the corner of the room. Xandie shuddered and avoided the rotting food, heading for the open suitcase. She rifled through but came up short. "Eric's a follower, not a leader. He's more concerned with food than anything else." *Time for the next room.*

Xandie peered out into the hallway before using Great-Aunt Rose's finger and unlocking and slipping into the next room.

An overpowering stench of jasmine slapped Xandie in the face, along with piles of lacy underwear spread over a neatly made bed. "Well, this isn't Mathilde's room. At least I hope not." Thankfully, Sofie didn't have half eaten plates of food attracting small fuzzy rodents. Xandie poked at the expensive underwear. "She's wishing." The muscled bear shifter had zero chance of getting anything male-related if she kept hanging out with Mathilde. The wizened bear shifter would scare any potential partner.

"Focus, Xandie." Ignoring the fancy underwear, Xandie rifled through Sofie's two suitcases but came up with nothing. Sliding a hand into a shallow pocket of the case, she pushed her hand deeper until she felt something teasing her fingertips. Carefully drawing it out, Xandie pursed her lips and read the name on the small business card.

"Tyr Greenhand." That supercilious fae got around, but why would Sofie have his card? Xandie slipped it back into place. She'd been searching long enough, she needed to get back to the dinner, or at least dessert. She had a feeling searching Mathilde's room would be pointless. That canny Elspeth nemesis wouldn't be caught dead with any sort of damning evidence in her room. Heading to the door, the glitter of something shiny on the bedside table drew her attention. Xandie poked at a silver bracelet with metal roses and thorns curled around the band. "Doesn't seem like Sofie's style."

In fact, it looked more like the ring Zach had given her. The same etching of roses around the band. And it resembled the jewelry Simon had for sale at the fair. Xandie prodded a metal thorn and hissed as the sharp edge drew blood. "It's as sharp as a weapon." Sucking the blood off her finger, Xandie stepped out of the room and headed downstairs. Reaching the hallway, she spotted a shadowy figure standing on the porch and the rough tones of her fiancé floated back. Xandie's heart melted. *How sweet, my beau is waiting for me.* Almost skipping, Xandie slipped out onto the porch, only to surprise cousin Sofie and Zach in a passionate kiss. "Do you have a death wish?"

The pair drew apart, and Zach shoved Sofie away, glaring at the female shifter. "What kind of prank was that?" He wiped away a smear of rose-pink lipstick from his cheek. He turned to Xandie, hands held up. "I know that looked bad, but it wasn't what you think."

"You mean, she didn't trick you out here and pretend she had something in her eye, then locked lips when she saw me?" Xandie countered. For a Harrow whose every breath invoked chaos and mayhem, the way-too-simple plan was obvious. Elspeth would be disgusted.

Zach rubbed a hand through his shaggy brown hair. "Okay. This is exactly what you think then."

Xandie arched an eyebrow. "Why don't you head inside while I talk to your cousin."

Zach cleared his throat and brushed Xandie's cheek with a kiss as he slipped past.

"And don't think we won't talk about you falling for such a pathetic scheme. I'm disappointed in you, Zach Braun," Xandie yelled over a shoulder as her fiancé left, before focusing on the smirking bear shifter.

"I can't help it if my weak American cousin wants me." Sofie let her muscular shoulder twitch in a nonchalant movement.

Xandie snorted. "Please. My grandmother is the wicked witch of Point Muse. She's an expert in manipulation. Your loser attempts are on the level of a toddler compared to her."

"You are..." Sofie fisted her hands and stiffened.

Xandie strolled forward and leaned against the porch column. The rose garden around the porch swelled with the scent of the flowers. "Yep. Me. The one who's marrying Zach and has this ring. Which is what you really want." Xandie waggled her ring at the bear and the roses next to her swayed along with the movement of her hand. Xandie turned her back on the freaky moving bushes and focused on Sofie. "Then you really aren't interested in him. You just want this ring. Why is that, little bear?"

Sofie jerked forward like a striking snake. "It's about family honor and our business. Something you know nothing about."

"Clocks, right? That's the Braun family business in the Black Forest?"

"It was. Now, thanks to your precious Zach's side of the family, and that black-hearted Goldi Locks, our family can't fight the ruin anymore. We need that ring back now." Sofie lunged at Xandie, hands outstretched.

Hecate's girded loins. No crazy bear shifter was taking her down. A whoosh of air zoomed past her, and a slice of hot pain on her cheek was all the warning she had before the garden slammed into Sofie. The blood red flowers, along with deep green stalks and vicious thorns, pinned the shrieking bear to the side of the inn.

"Not something you see every day." Xandie shook her head, eyes wide. From whining about Goldi Locks and bad luck to death by roses. Elspeth couldn't have planned it better.

"I will kill you for this. Do you hear me?" Sofie batted at a rose as it curled its way along her jaw before effectively gagging her with flora.

"I see you are finally able to access the benefits of the ring. *Surprising.*" The tall, silver-haired fae stepped out onto the porch. "I felt the magic explode, and I must say, I didn't expect such an effective use of its power." He arched an eyebrow and looked Xandie up and down. "Quite surprising."

"What?" The ring had done this? Xandie lifted a hand and stared at the peeling, unattractive black and silver ring with roses etched around the band. *Roses.* The ring had responded to Sofie's attack and protected her.

"The ring belongs to Milady Greenhand. It has been missing long enough. Even if it responds to you, it's of fae design and make and belongs on another's hand. The rightful owner."

Smelled like a clue to her. "If it's fae, then why does a bear shifter clan have it?"

"Fate and the machinations of thieving humans. Unless you're here to discuss terms, I think I will turn in." He spun toward the door.

"Why do so many people want it? For its magic powers? And how do I make it work? I'm supposed to be immune to magic as the Librarian."

"Humans. Always full of questions." Tyr paused at the front door. "The ring will only work in fae hands normally, but possibly your connection to the Library opens you up to higher magic. Fate is fickle. We'll never know why it responded to you." He opened the door, and a pool of artificial light lit his silver hair. "Of course, not every half breed fae lurking in the area can be trusted to look after the ring's best interest. That has now become your job. Guard it well until you make your decision on its final ownership, Librarian." Tyr Greenhand disappeared into the inn as Xandie's family, and all the Braun shifters, surged onto the porch, staring dumbfounded at a rose trussed Sofie.

Elspeth cackled, and light throughout the inn flared and fizzled, causing yells and curses. "Now that's what I call an end to a family dinner. Couldn't have planned it better myself." Xandie's grandmother slapped her on the back. "Have I told you you're my favorite granddaughter?"

Lucky me...

NINE

"I don't understand the necessity of inviting others. I'm sure we can handle any research activities needed." Theo, black feline guardian to the Supernatural Great Library of Alexandria, twitched his whiskers.

"Superiority complex much?"

"I. Am. A. Feline."

"True." Xandie raised a hand and snatched a flying scroll out of the air. Soft, glowing lights flickered overhead in an erratic pattern, like a child playing with a light. "Very funny, Library." The Great Library of Alexandria might be an ancient repository for all supernatural knowledge, but it also had the attention span and humor of a toddler. Xandie carefully placed the scroll in a pile ready for shelving. Like Doctor Who's TARDIS, the Library was bigger on the inside and could manipulate its own dimensions to make more space. Her job as the Librarian was to create order out of the chaos, make sure all visitors received the correct information, and record all appointments in the special ledger the Library provided. Xandie closed her eyes and inhaled, the musty smell of a normal Library absent. Instead, the

Library infused the room with a faint scent of roses. "Roses?" Xandie's eyes snapped open, and she quickly made sure no rampaging flora with thorns had tied Theo to the wall.

"You have a floral craving?"

"Roses kind of attacked that Sofie bear. Held her against the wall of the inn after she kissed Zach." Xandie paced up and down in the center of the room, dodging the gleaming wooden desks and comfortable chairs dotted around the room.

"Ooh, gossip." Theo settled down on the ground, dislodging the chittering pet imp, Horatio, from his back in the process. "Do tell?"

Xandie glared at Theo. "There's nothing to tell. The bear wench tricked him, and he fell for it. She just wanted to get a reaction out of me."

"And boy, did she get one. I've never been so proud as when I saw that shifter pinned to the wall by flora." Elspeth stood framed in the Library doorway, Colin cradled in her arms.

"It's not like I did it on purpose. In fact, I have no clue how I did it at all."

Elspeth dumped her pug minion onto a chair as she sauntered up to Xandie. Grabbing her hand, the wicked witch of Point Muse held the beringed hand aloft. "Not exactly pretty, is it?"

"It wasn't this black before. I have no clue what the jeweler did to it. But you can see where the black is flaking off like old paint. There are etched roses poking through."

"Someone should take Elspeth's moped license away." Melody Braun, bear shifter, Zach's younger sister, and police deputy, stumbled through the Library door and collapsed, panting, on a couch. Her short, light brown hair stood up in tangled clumps, and her face looked like it had been permanently stained bright red to match her bloodshot eyes.

Elspeth dropped Xandie's hand and sneered in the general direction of the bear. "Just you try and take it from me, fuzz."

"Actually, I don't think she even has an official license. She just bought the hot pink moped off the internet and started delivering pizzas with it. Although that didn't last long." Holly wandered across and settled on a small chair near Xandie's desk.

"I got bored." Elspeth shrugged.

"I think she was just trying to copy my silver moped."

Narrowing her gaze on her granddaughter, Elspeth pointed an iridescent green painted nail. "Pull my finger. I dare you."

Holly shuddered. "No thanks. Last time I took you up on your offer, you zapped me like you had a taser, and I was out for hours. You probably changed my heart rhythms. I should make an appointment for a general health check."

"Why did you invite the hypochondriac along for a family pow wow? Couldn't you have asked the one who cooks? At least we'd have snacks with the whine."

Poking out her tongue, Holly adjusted her position on the chair and resolutely ignored her grandmother. "Everyone will just have to cope with a banshee funeral attendant instead of the baker. Lila's up at the fair organizing catering, then she's back at the bakery."

Holly worked at the Elysian Fields Funeral Home. She loved it, but the job and her banshee nature promoted a somewhat morbid edge to her sarcasm.

"I'll catch Lila up later. For now, let's focus on the fact my ring is magic and everyone wants it."

Melody started a slow clap. "I applaud your Sofie

restraint method last night. She's getting on everyone's nerves. Her and the whole Black Forest contingent. Mum is just glad they're up at the inn and not staying at Braun Lodge. She'd have buried them out back by the creek by now."

Xandie dropped onto the couch next to a slumbering Colin. "I heard Sofie talking about the ring to Ernest Gem and someone else I couldn't see. They both mentioned the ring, and Sofie blathered on about restoring family honor with it. But that fae guy, Greenhand, mentioned it was fae jewelry. So how did it get into the German Brauns' hands?"

Melody waved a hand tipped with brightly colored nails in the air. "I can answer that." She took a deep breath and recited in a singsong voice. "Once upon a time, a group of peaceful cuckoo clock-building bear shifters lived in a lovely bear compound in a thick forest. They loved their clock-making and were very prosperous. Then one day a thieving Goldi Locks broke in and robbed them blind. A tussle ensued. And the patriarch of the family didn't make it. Goldie got sent to the slammer for murder and breaking and entering, but as the bears buried their leader, they found clutched in his hands a silver ring. Taking it as their due for losing their patriarch, it was kept as an heirloom and passed down until one son decided to head to the new world. The reigning leader of the clan at the time gifted his son with the ring in case he found a suitable bear bride in the new world. The end." Melody drew a breath before slumping back onto the chair. "The bears left behind hated the fact my ancestor got the ring and have moaned about bad luck ever since. Seriously, I don't know why it's such a big deal. It didn't even belong to us in the first place."

Xandie scratched the top of her nose, which had begun to tingle, and considered her eyesore of a ring. "That man at the inn said it was of fae design and belonged to a fae. So how did Goldi Locks get it?"

Elspeth rolled her eyes. "Obviously, she stole it from the fae who owned it, or..." Elspeth paced in a circle, spinning around and around with a stamp of her tiny feet. "Or the little light-fingered rat filched it from the fae smith who made it."

"That makes more sense." Melody nodded. "The Brauns certainly didn't have it before the patriarch tussled with Goldi. He grabbed it off the thieving murderess before he died, and she stole it from someone else. Talk about a circle of life."

"And the fae from the inn tried to buy the ring for his boss, Rosalind Greenhand." Xandie held up the ring with etched rose designs peeking through the peeling black surface. "Think the roses on this are a coincidence?"

Elspeth snorted. "No such thing as coincidences. What else did that pointy-eared, snooty-pants have to say?"

"Just to be careful the ring doesn't fall into the wrong hands." Xandie snapped her fingers. "He did say something about half-faes in the area wanting it too." She raised her voice. "Library? Information on a silver ring with roses etched around the band. Probably designed and owned by a fae owner. Also, names of any half-faes who live near Point Muse currently."

"Don't forget about the Locks family. Best have ammunition when they come looking for that cursed piece of jewelry." Elspeth smirked. "Of course, I'm always here to back you up...*for a price*. But it doesn't hurt to have a little bit of a secret weapon, just in case."

"You think they will?"

Elspeth shrugged. "Their family business is thieving,

and this is a goodie that got away. Of course they'll come hunting for it."

Theo sneezed and rolled over, narrowly missing squishing Horatio, his imp. "All that talk about heists and stolen jewelry. You forgot one thing…"

"Man, I woke up at the wrong time. I thought I'd sleep through all the yapping and wake up to snacks." Colin shivered and sat up. His mouth opened wide in a large yawn.

"Excuse me, but adults are talking." Theo flapped his tail at Elspeth's mouthy pug. "As I was saying, the evidence of possible multiple suspects was just given to you by the bear and the moody dark witch."

"Just spit it out, fuzzball. I ain't getting any younger, and my stomach is getting empty."

"Could we stop the minion snark and get to the good bits please?" Some days, the squabbles between her cat guardian and Elspeth's manufactured crime-against-nature evil pug drove her to silent screaming.

"Fine." Theo heaved a sigh. "Two obvious points. The ring has roses etched on it and it was originally commissioned by a fae." Theo waited with an expectant expression and then rolled his eyes. "It's obvious the fae at Mayweather Inn works for the original owner."

"We pretty much worked that out. And the second?"

"That Goldi Locks thief? Know anyone at the fair who might have a talent for thievery with the last name of Locks?"

"Charlie Locks." Holly nodded. "I thought there was something off about her. No one should be that perky. It's just wrong."

"I'd also already worked that out, *and* she was accused of stealing at the fair," Xandie offered her addition to the conversation.

"I like that kid. She's got moxie."

"I don't like moxie. I prefer moldable and silent. That's where I failed with you girls. Besides, if that Locks girl had just plain thieving on her agenda, she'd have stripped the fair clean and been gone with her ill-gotten goods already. She's staying for a reason. Mark my words, that too-perky composure hides hidden depths. I'd watch her carefully."

"She's not the only one we're watching. I saw Simon Wald hand off packages to different people at the fair. I'm pretty sure he's the one who tipped off Sabine that Charlie had been stealing. He also seemed pretty shocked when the mob didn't find anything. Like he'd set her up."

"Ah, mobs." Elspeth smiled dreamily. "I remember the mobs from the good old days."

"You should. The last time you tried to outrun one on a purloined mobility scooter, we found a dead body. My Librarian had to solve the whole mess you created." Theo jumped up and waited as his imp climbed onto the cat's furry back. The imp held on tight as Theo pranced through the center of the room.

Colin eyed the cat and imp and scrambled off the couch. "The furry brainiac has a point. My dame does like a good mob. Say, when was the last time the Librarian went shopping?" He trotted behind Theo as the two left the room squabbling.

"Now we have Sofie, the fae at the inn, Charlie Locks, and Simon the silversmith as suspects," Xandie said. "Couldn't we just have one suspect for once?"

Melody cleared her throat. "I have the next few days off. I can tail Simon and Charlie. I need to practice my undercover work anyway." She winked.

"And tall, blond Simon isn't exactly hard on the eyes."

"The bad ones are always attractive." Elspeth pursed

her lips and fluffed her cotton-candy-colored curly wig. "I should know." She cackled, and the lights overhead remained steady. The wicked witch pouted. "I hate this Library. It could at least let me play once in a while."

Holly stood and stretched. "There's only room for one head honcho here and that's the Library." She pointed at Melody. "You want a lift, bear, or do I leave you to Elspeth's crazed driving again?"

Jumping up, Melody squeezed Holly in a bear hug. "Thank you. My sanity salutes you."

Elspeth rolled her eyes. "Everyone's a critic. Well, now I guess we've been more helpful than the Library. One to me." Elspeth sauntered out, in search of a missing minion.

"For once, she's right." Xandie patted the desk. "You okay, Library? Normally the information flies out at me as soon as I ask." The lights overhead took on a rosy glow, and a small pile of bound books on a shelf close to Xandie's desk rattled. "Aha. You already had the information put aside for me. Why not give them to me in front of the others?" The lights flickered but stayed rosy. Xandie took a shot in the dark. "You didn't want to embarrass or upset Melody?" The lights flickered wildly before settling down to a normal, subtle glow. Xandie patted her desk again. "Melody would never care, but it was nice of you to think of her."

Grabbing the books, Xandie settled in and flicked through the first one, a slim, blue, leather-bound book, with only four chapters to it. "Not a lot of information in this one." She flicked through the pages, giggling at the childlike images within. "Looks like Melody was right about Goldilocks or Goldi Locks, since that's her real name." Xandie paused at the mention of a fae, the smith who'd originally crafted the ring before Goldie had stolen it. "Hello, Albert Schwartzwald of the Black Forest." The image in front of her depicted a grizzled, thickly muscled fae with a tidy beard and solid gray eyes.

Something familiar about the fae smith nagged at Xandie. She pursed her lips, trying to puzzle it out, but gave up. Her Librarian brain would release the answer when she needed it. She looked at the final two tomes in the pile, both history books. One, the history of the nefarious Locks clan and the other on the holdings of the Greenhand clan. Cracking her knuckles, Xandie settled in for a night of heavy reading.

It wasn't always about the action and the body count. Sometimes good old research saved the day—and Elspeth—from going to jail.

TEN

"If you don't close your yap, you'll catch flies." Colin licked the icing off the cupcake and then tossed the rest to a panting hellhound.

Xandie blinked her eyes rapidly after a bone-crunching yawn. "It's early. Be nice. I was up late researching last night."

"Then you need copious amounts of sugar." Lila placed a steaming mug of hot chocolate in front of her cousin, along with a plate of tiny little coffee cakes. "Try my perk-you-up coffee cakes. Should give you some energy."

Smiling gratefully, Xandie devoured one of the cakes in a single bite. A shiver of energy spread its way from her stomach to her throat, and her eyes widened. "Wow. These are great." Lila's witchy Harrow gifts were poured into her baking. There was a reason Point Muse loved Lila's bakery. Thankfully, Xandie had managed to snag a table in the morning rush. Well, thanks to Colin hovering near the table, nobody had dared sit down. Everyone was too scared of Elspeth. *Speaking of...* "Elspeth's supposed to be joining me for breakfast before we head to the fair. Have you seen her?"

Lila rolled her eyes and shoved her curly brown ponytail over one shoulder. "She was here when I came downstairs. Matthew, the traitor, let her in." Lila eyed her unrepentant boyfriend as he stood smirking behind Xandie's chair. "She's currently pretending to ice slices, but she's in one of her moods. So, watch out."

Colin licked a blob of pink icing off his cheek. "Yeah, watch my lady today. She woke up bored this morning. Not enough action."

Xandie froze, a little cake halfway to her mouth.

Lila squeaked and grabbed her hellhound's collar.

Matthew Grim, Lila's boyfriend and the resident reaper of Point Muse, gripped the back of the chair next to Xandie. "Bored? She woke up bored?" His manly voice squeaked on the last word.

Colin snorted. "Why do you think I'm out here instead of in the kitchen with freshly baked goods? I love my girl, but she's a terror in orthopedic shoes when she's bored." The pug shuddered. "No one deserves that. Not even my cuddly magnificence."

The reaper swallowed, his face pale. "On second thought, I'm not that hungry. I'll eat at lunch or maybe even dinner."

"Don't be such a baby. Sit your patootie down. I slaved over a hot kitchen all morning for you all." Elspeth slammed a large plate of mini crab cakes next to Lila's coffee cakes.

"You mean I slaved, and you stood next to me the whole time telling me I wasn't making them correctly."

"My recipe so I get to delegate as I see fit." Elspeth beamed and waited for her family to move.

The conversations at the other tables in the bakery died

down to a murmur as the packed shop watched the wicked witch of Point Muse's every move.

"Well?" Elspeth glared at her family, pushing them into action.

Xandie grabbed a crab cake as Lila hurried to the table and Matthew scrambled into a chair.

Colin snuck under the table, Nash, the hellhound, joining him. "Just drop some crabcakes under here. I'm safe from direct fire if I stay out of sight."

"The pug's got the right idea," Matthew whispered under his breath.

Xandie widened her eyes. "Ixnay on the speaking back...ay."

"Just eat. Don't look her in the eyes. We don't want a dominance battle. It could rip the town in half," Lila mumbled around her mouthful of crab.

Matthew dropped his eyes and focused on the food. "It looks delicious, Elspeth. Really nice. Much better than Lila's food." He sent his girlfriend an apologetic look.

Lila just shrugged. "Every man, woman, and child for themselves when Elspeth's bored. Do what you need to survive."

Xandie took a large bite of the crab cakes and swallowed quickly. "That's delicious. I praise the writer of the recipe. All hail crab cakes."

"Mmm," Lila hummed her agreement.

Elspeth clapped her hands and the whole room sagged in relief.

Xandie risked looking up. The bakery was packed, everyone loading up before heading to the fair. Even Milly from the fair committee stood waiting at the counter. Xandie gave a little wave as the woman looked over with a smile. Not so long ago, Lila had been terrified her business would go under when the Devlin twins across the road opened their dessert bakery. But the opposite had happened. The two bakeries fit together. Both had seen an increase in business. A win-win situation.

"What *are* those sad little things?" Sofie Braun and her older brother, Eric, stood by the side of the table. The female bear held a hand over her nose. "What a horrible stench. You really serve that kind of food here? I'm shocked."

"Incoming." Colin's voice echoed from underneath the table.

"Excuse me?" Elspeth's amber eyes flashed, and her fiery red wig with matching long red braids seemed to catch on fire, glowing brightly.

Waving a hand in front of her face, Sofie fake gagged. "The substandard food served here in Point Muse wouldn't be tolerated back home."

Eric extended a hand. "Maybe I should test one, to see how bad it is?"

Slapping her brother's hand away, Sofie shook her head. "Don't try the food. It will make you sick. We have a big day today." The bear beamed at the Harrows and Lila's boyfriend. "Why, Matthew. How nice to see you again. I didn't take enough time at the family dinner to talk to you."

"If he knows what's good for him, he'll never talk to you again." Lila glared at her boyfriend. "Right, Matthew, dear?"

Matthew's gaze bounced from witch to bear shifter. The reaper cleared his throat. "I think I'm going to be very busy over the next few days."

Elspeth snorted. "Way to stand up for yourself, reaper." Xandie's grandmother glared at the female shifter. "You seem like you have something to say, and it isn't about my crab cakes. Spit it out, monobrow."

Sofie's hand drifted to her eyebrows before she dropped it and scowled at the wicked witch. "Fine. You need to give me the ring back now, Librarian. It doesn't belong to you."

Xandie blew her breath out. She was heartily sick of talking about the ugly thing. "This ring?" Xandie held a hand up. The raised amber jewel in the center caught the light, which made the black peeling spots look even worse.

"See?" Sophie exploded and poked her brother, who was still staring at the crab cakes. "She's ruined it. The ring hates her so much it's peeling."

"Maybe people should stop trying to take it off me. Especially when it doesn't belong to them."

"That piece of jewelry belongs to the Black Forest side of the family. Not some Librarian." Sofie took a step toward Xandie. Her shoulders bunched, a small hump formed between her shoulder blades, and the monobrow Elspeth mentioned earlier suddenly rippled across her forehead.

Xandie pushed her chair back. She'd reached her limit with this woman. "I did some research last night. The only reason you have the ring is that Goldi Locks robbed some poor silversmith and left it behind when she tussled with your family. Doesn't even belong to you."

Baring jagged teeth, Sofie hissed, "Our ancestor died, and that ring is our blood payment. And ever since that traitor Braun stole it and ran to America, our side of the family has suffered. It's not happening anymore. We *will* have that ring, give it to its rightful owner, and repair our family honor and fortune."

"Give it? Or sell it?" So much for restoring family honor. Xandie curled her lip. It wasn't hard to see the youngest Braun was out for a large payday at everybody else's expense.

"*Why you...*" Sophie surged forward, claws extended.

"Whoa there." Matthew leapt to his feet and placed himself between the women. Lila, at his side, glared at the out-of-control bear.

"Pack it in, Sofie. You aren't getting my ring, ever," Xandie yelled from behind the tall, solid, reaper's back. "Maybe I'll sell it first. I'm sure I can find a buyer for it."

"Over my dead body."

"That could be arranged," Xandie sneered back.

"And to think I was bored this morning." Elspeth clapped her hands, glee evident in her wide grin. Her red wig had settled down to a muted shade instead of a fiery glow.

Milly sidled over to Xandie and put an arm around her. "Why don't we head out to the kitchen and calm down. There's no point arguing with a bear when they have their hump out."

"That's right, run away. Just don't expect her to watch your back. What's that saying? Keep your friends close and your enemies closer?" Sofie glared at Milly.

"Okay. That's it." Lila folded her arms across her chest. "I'm banning you."

Sofie scoffed. "You and what army, Harrow?"

"I don't need an army. I have him." Lila pointed over her shoulder at her hellhound who'd emerged from under the table. Her rapidly growing, growling, red-eyed hellhound that now stood at the height of a small pony.

"Run, hairy meat," Nash growled, and a trickle of smoke drifted out of one nostril.

Finally dragging his gaze away from the crab cakes, Eric grabbed Sofie's arm. He towed her away. "I think you made your point, sister. Time to leave before we become dog food." He shoved her out the door, letting it slam shut behind him.

Elspeth cackled, and shadows writhed around the room, dodging the silent, staring patrons. "Breakfast and a show. It doesn't get any better than that."

"I could have taken her."

"Of course, you could have. You're a Librarian." Milly patted Xandie's back. "You're fierce and quite interesting, and I think all the Harrows are a delight."

"You're about the only one who thinks that." Xandie kicked a stone as she walked through the middle of the fair. Taking a breather in the kitchen hadn't helped, but a burst of fresh air had. She couldn't believe she'd let that mouthy bear get to her.

"Take the compliment, dear. It's not often I give them out. Now what will you do about the ring?"

"Ring. Ring. Ring. All about the bling, or not so bling at the moment." Xandie sighed. "Whatever Sofie said, it doesn't belong to her. I'll talk to my fiancé, but it really isn't ours to keep."

"You're more logical and reasonable than I expected you to be." Milly considered Xandie, head cocked to one side.

"It's the Harrow blood. It confuses people."

"Possibly, but still food for thought." Milly patted Xandie on the arm. "Why don't you go visit your mother? She's in the main tent with a knife."

Xandie brightened. "That's a great idea, Milly." With a wave, she hot footed to the main tent and her mother. Flipping the tent flap open, Xandie blinked, not expecting such a bright light to greet her.

"It's for my knife throwing. I need a clear line of sight." Miranda beamed at her daughter and gave her a tight hug. "I heard about your run-in with that bear. I'm so proud of you for standing up for yourself."

"Might have lost my temper," Xandie admitted.

Miranda pinched Xandie's cheek. "You get that from my side of the family. Most Harrows do have a temper." She linked arms with her daughter and strolled toward the large round target set in the middle of the tent. "How about helping me out with my knife act and being my assistant? I have a show in a little while, and the normal helper hasn't turned up."

"Uh." Xandie laughed nervously. Her mother's skill with different weapons was unparalleled. But knife throwing wasn't on Xandie's bucket list.

"It'll be fine, sweetie. A mother-daughter bonding moment." Excitement glistened in Miranda's amber eyes.

Giving in, Xandie pressed herself up against the target. "Fine, but if you kill me, I'll haunt you."

"Of course, dear. I wouldn't expect anything else from a Harrow." Miranda patted Xandie on the cheek. She quickly strapped her daughter's arms out at an angle. "Now, there's no need to worry. I am an expert. Just don't move."

"Not an issue." Xandie trusted her mother's skills... But with her luck lately?

"Just be glad I'm not using the spinning wheel of death." Miranda grimaced. "No one wants to be upside down having knives thrown at them." Xandie's mother strode to a small table lined with knives. "Now, these are all specially weighted, so the knife will come close but will come down and the tip will angle away from you. Makes the knife look like it's come closer to you than it actually has." Xandie's mother picked up a knife and balanced it on her palm. "Your grandmother gave me these for my birthday. She has exquisite taste."

"Yep, all I got you were flowers. I can see that was a mistake now."

Miranda giggled, then sobered. "We need a few practices before we get the crowd in. Are you ready?"

"As I'll ever be."

Nodding, Miranda lined the target up and let fly.

The knife sailed past Xandie's cheek, her hair blowing against her face from the force of the tip hitting the target next to her.

"See? Nothing to it. Let's do another." Miranda quickly chose another knife and threw it in one swift move.

The blade flew toward Xandie, but instead of veering down at the last moment, the metal sliced past Xandie's ear and embedded into the board and her hair.

Xandie squeaked as blood trickled down her jaw, trailing onto her neck.

"Hecate's cursed toenails." Miranda rushed forward. "I'm so sorry, sweetie. That shouldn't have happened." She released Xandie's hands and yanked the knife out. Dropping it to the ground, she grabbed a clean rag out of her pocket and held it to Xandie's ear. "It's just a scratch, but anywhere in the head tends to bleed profusely."

Wincing, Xandie grabbed the rag and held it pressed to her ear. "It's okay, Mom. Everyone has an off day. It's only a scratch anyway."

Shaking her head, Miranda frowned. "Not me. It's my business to be accurate. I have no clue how the knife scratched you. It's like its trajectory changed the closer it drew to the board."

"And me. As it got closer to me." Xandie stepped away from the board, fighting the chill that settled in her bones. Her mother seemed adamant the knife shouldn't have cut her. Maybe she was right? "Mom? Did you check the board after you put it up and before you volunteered me for your knife assistant?"

"A good workman always checks his tools, so of course I did. But I grabbed a coffee after I set it up. I was only gone for five minutes."

Maybe someone had sabotaged the board? Ducking around the back, Xandie ran a hand over the board. A clicking noise reached her ears as she pressed down on a small, raised button. A flap popped open. "Mom? Is there supposed to be a secret compartment?"

"Yes. It's a feature of this board. Why?"

Reaching her hand in, Xandie drew out a small, brown, hessian bag and held it up. "Because I think we were hexed."

Someone had just tried to kill me. Another typical day in Point Muse...

ELEVEN

"It's just a scratch. I'm not scarred for life."

"It's a scratch from one of my knives. Your life could have been very short." Miranda paced the length of the first-aid tent.

Xandie winced as a healer swabbed the cut with disinfectant. She poked the woman in the arm. "Tell my mother I'll live."

Sighing, the healer placed the disinfectant on the table and focused on the worried mother. "She's not at Hades' door. She's not going to lose her ear or faint from blood loss. In fact, it's so small, it's a waste of my time to heal it. I've swabbed the scratch and given her a tetanus potion. Now could you please leave my tent? You're giving me a headache with all the pacing."

"See?" Xandie slid off the table and flipped her hair over her injured ear. "How about we focus less on my impending death and more on the moron who placed that hex bag on the target?"

Blowing out a breath, Miranda gathered herself and followed Xandie out of the tent. "Sorry I lost it. You're precious to me. The idea that one of my knives cut you...could have killed you..." She trailed off and shivered.

"Makes you lose your mind. I get it." Xandie patted her mother's lean, muscled back. For years after protecting Xandie and being chased off a cliff by a killer knight, Xandie's mother had lost her memory. The only thing she remembered was the need to protect Xandie. Even with her memories back, that need still drove her mother. "I promise, I'm fine. If I feel faint, I'll tell you. Right now, I need answers."

Miranda nodded; a faint smile edged the corners of her lips. "Sometimes you remind me of myself. Go ahead, ask your questions."

Xandie led her mother through the fair, opting for a secluded picnic table for her interview. "How did you get the knife throwing job? I thought it would be a specialized job only an expert could do?"

"The fair has a regular knife thrower, but he reported sick just before the fair moved to Point Muse."

"What kind of sick?"

"A scratch that became infected, I believe." She looked pointedly at her daughter. "Scratches can be dangerous."

Xandie waved away her mother's concern. "Who appointed you as the knife thrower?"

"I think the Point Muse fair committee put some suggestions forward and management decided, along with some of the long-term fair employees."

"So, Simon Wald, the silversmith, would have been one of those voters?"

Miranda nodded. "Possibly. But if you're thinking it was to get me in place to get at you, how would they have known you'd volunteer to be my knife assistant?"

"I didn't exactly volunteer," Xandie mumbled under her breath, then cleared her throat as her mother glared.

"Why didn't your regular knife assistant turn up?"

"She left me a note telling me she felt sick just before you turned up. I was planning to track down Sabine to scare up a replacement."

"Someone would have known I was scheduled to be the floater today. And, of course, why wouldn't a daughter want to visit her mother? There's a lot of variables to consider."

Miranda's eyes misted over. "You remind me so much of myself."

"Who knew a tough, black ops agent could get so emotional?" Xandie gave her mother a quick hug. "But I need my focused mother back. Someone wanted me hurt, or worse."

"Because of your ring?" Her mother tapped the discolored jewelry. "There seems to be a heightened interest in the piece. That would indicate it's valuable, or at least valuable to someone in some way."

"Everything does seem to be centered around it." Xandie wiggled her fingers, letting the sun hit the metal. The rose motifs were barely visible through the peeling black gunk coated over it. The special properties of the ring had definitely come in handy. And after the research in the Library, she was positive the fae who'd owned it originally was Lady Rosalind Greenhand. The fae at the inn's boss. Xandie had a feeling there was more at play than a noble wanting their bling back. Decision made, she jumped up and pointed at her mother. "You need to get back to your act, and I need to hunt down your sick knife assistant."

"I think I'll stay with you. You might need me."

"No. You need to carry on as normally as possible.

Flush out anyone overly interested in your act. You just need to find another assistant first."

"Oh, that's handled. Mother volunteered to help when the committee suggested I step in. She's always loved playing with shiny, sharp things. She'll jump at the offer to be my knife assistant, and she's skulking around the fair somewhere anyway."

Xandie shuddered. "The last thing any sane person needs, supernatural or otherwise, is for Elspeth to develop a hankering for sharp weapons. But if that's what you want, you go play with knives, and I'll track down the sick assistant."

"She has a lilac van with daisies painted on the side. You can't miss it."

Blowing her mother a kiss, Xandie made a beeline straight to the fair's residential vans. And smack bang in the middle was a daisy decorated one. Pulling up short in front of it, Xandie took a breath, calming her nerves before grilling her witness.

"You constipated?"

"Argh." Xandie jumped to the side with a small shriek.

Colin barked out a rough laugh. "Man, you kids are nervous nellies. A good scare could send you young Harrows straight into orbit."

"We have a healthy fear response. Living with Elspeth does that to a person. What are you doing here?"

"Elspeth is gonna have fun with knives this morning, so I decided to see why you were scuttling around the fair. Plus, you might have snacks."

Xandie patted her jeans pocket. "Nope. No snacks here. Find Lila — I'm sure she has something put aside for you already."

"The lady hiding in the van might, and she's closer."

Colin pawed the door. "Saw the skinny chick creeping around before Miranda got her steel out."

"I thought the assistant was supposed to be sick?"

"Looked okay to me. Girlie needs a good meal and some meat on her bones, but she didn't look like she was suffering from the plague." Colin shoved a shoulder against the door. "Oi. Knife Girl. You got any snacks?" The door swung open, and Colin tumbled back off the step. He shook himself and growled at the woman blocking the doorway. "I definitely better get some quality snacks out of this. You crazy dame. You could have ruined my pugnificence."

"Excuse me?" A tall, skinny woman with a shock of bright blue hair and a thin, reedy voice stared bewildered at the investigating duo.

Xandie sighed. "We get that a lot. He grows on you like a fungus." She dredged up a smile. "I'm Xandie Meyers. I'm the Librarian and the floater for the fair today. I was wondering if I could ask you a few questions?"

The young woman wrapped her baby pink dressing gown around herself. "Look, I don't know anything. I need to get back to bed. I'm sick." She coughed into her arm.

"Sorry, doll face, but that was pathetic. I've been scammed by the best so I should know." Colin surged up the stairs and between the woman's legs, sending her flying back inside the van.

"Oops." Xandie would have to take Colin to her interviews more often. Stepping into the van, Xandie closed the door behind her. She scrutinized the interior of the van and its owner. Little Miss Knife Assistant didn't look too sick, and the half empty chocolate box on the table indicated her appetite was just fine. The inside of the small van had costumes and props strewn around, and fake costume jewelry was piled on the counter. Off to one side, a lovely silver cross on a velvet ribbon lay shining. Now, that piece didn't look like a costume and seemed very familiar. Following a hunch, Xandie picked up the cross. "This is so pretty. Been after one just like it." She ran her hand over the lightly engraved metal and accidentally depressed a small bump on the base. With a tiny whirring noise, a sharp stiletto knife slid out. "My goodness. My mother would love that. Can I ask where you got it from?"

The young woman carefully yanked the cross away from Xandie and pushed the bump again. The blade slid back inside. "It was a gift. I have no clue where it came from." She stowed the cross in a drawer and smoothed her hair, flustered. "Why are you in my van again?"

Someone didn't want to talk about the murderous jewelry. Xandie was positive she'd seen something similar at Simon's store. "You didn't turn up at work today. Why?"

The knife assistant wrapped her arms around her waist. "I'm sick. I told you. I didn't want to infect anyone." She shifted and pretended to wipe her nose with a dry tissue.

Xandie took a leaf out of Elspeth's playbook. "Colin? Did you have tuna this morning for breakfast?"

"Huh?" Colin looked confused before he caught on to Xandie's plan. "Why, yes. Yes, I did, Alexandra. Along with one of Elspeth's crab cakes. Why do you ask?"

"I'm just worried about your stomach issues. This is a small van, and your issues with seafood are famous in Point Muse. I'd hate for you to ruin this pretty little van." Xandie smirked. Using Colin as a threatened weapon of mass olfactory destruction was kind of fun.

"Fine." The woman threw her hands up. "I'm not sick."

"No kidding. Why throw a sickie today?"

"I got an anonymous note asking me to call in sick at the last moment. It came along with the cross."

"Why would you want to do what a strange note tells you to do?"

"Are you kidding me? Do you know how much this is worth?" The knife assistant pointed to the half empty box of chocolates. "Whoever it was gave me chocolate and jewelry. Plus, I get a day off. It wasn't hard to go along with it. Besides, our normal knife thrower isn't here." She wrinkled her nose. "I hate training new throwers."

"What happened to the regular one?"

"He had a big bender and came back with a nasty scratch. Next thing I know, he was sick, and the scratch was infected." She shuddered. "It looked disgusting. He stayed back at our last stop to get it treated, but..." Her voice trailed off, and she had an uncertain look on her face.

"But what?"

"Edwin swore he'd barely had anything to drink, but he couldn't even remember the night or how he got the scratch."

Sounds like someone had been hexed. This was all part of a plan. A plan for Miranda to take his place and for Xandie to end up injured or worse. Simon had shown interest in the ring before, had access to the main tent, and that cross looked like his work. But what kind of motive did he have to kill her jeweler and hurt Xandie? Was it all still about the ring? Xandie stood and motioned to Colin. "Thanks for answering my questions."

The girl shrugged. "I didn't have much choice. Are you going to speak to that scary Sabine about me faking?"

"Nope." Xandie shook her head. "I try to avoid her and her clipboard. She scares me."

"Ditto."

Xandie nodded thanks and let Colin out into the morning sunlight.

"Did you get what you needed, kid?" Colin pranced beside Xandie as she headed for the catering tent.

"I have a few ideas now."

"Good. How about we swing past Lila and grab some breakfast?"

"Haven't you already eaten?"

"Second breakfast then. That's a thing, right?"

Xandie rolled her eyes. The pug's life was ruled by his stomach urges.

Charlie slipped up next to Xandie and clapped her hands. "What did you learn? Bribed, right? I'm betting on being bribed. Something blingy or sweet or both. Am I right? I'm right."

Perky should be outlawed. "Why do you say bribed?"

Charlie rolled her eyes. "Normal knife thrower's out sick. Your mother is in, then her assistant turns up sick too. She ropes you in and you get sliced. Doesn't take an expert to work out what happened."

"Just out of curiosity, how did you hear about the mishap with the knife?" Xandie narrowed her eyes on the blonde, Shirley-Temple-curly-haired juggler. Charlie Locks had hidden layers. Had she learned that from her criminal mastermind family?

"You're an expert on dodgy undertakings, aren't you, Locks?" Sofie Braun stepped out from behind a van, her hands loose at her side.

"Some things are more obvious than others, she-bear." Charlie still skipped but the skin around her eyes had tightened.

Xandie braced herself for forthcoming mayhem.

"What's obvious to me, thief, is that you're here to finish what that killer, Goldi Locks, started." Sofie bared her teeth and stepped into the girl's path.

Colin detoured around the shifter and sat watching the women.

Charlie's smirk dropped away. "I have nothing to do with Goldi Locks' vendetta against your family."

"Since when? The Locks clan has always gone out of its way to make every Braun's life a misery. Your family is the reason our cuckoo clock business is failing. You won't get the ring. I'll see you, and whoever gets in my way, dead first." Sofie jabbed a finger into Charlie's forehead. "Got it?"

"Take your claws off my head," Charlie sweetly demanded.

Sofie flicked a sharpened tip against bare skin. "Or what, pipsqueak? What are you going to do? Eat my porridge?"

"How about you eat dirt?" Charlie slapped Sofie's claws out of the way and swept a leg through the shifter's. She knocked the bear back a step or two. Unfortunately, Colin still hadn't moved, and the Braun youngster tripped over the pug and hit the ground with an audible crunch.

Sofie roared, the noise echoing around the fair.

"Why do I always find my fiancée near a downed body?"

Xandie winced as her fiancé *and* police chief strode into view. "At least she isn't dead."

This is Point Muse. It could get far, far worse...

TWELVE

"Let me get this straight." Zach Braun rubbed the back of his head. "You dumped a shifter, twice your size and weight, on their back because she flicked your forehead with a claw? Did I get that right?"

Charlie nodded, her top knot ponytail bobbing. "That's exactly what happened. It was a flick with *intent*. You gonna take me to the slammer?" The little juggler leaned her head on her hand and pouted. "Orange isn't my color."

"I'm not arresting you. Just asking a few questions to clarify the situation."

"In *my* catering tent." Lila glared, hands on hips, at the policeman and the juggler. "We *do* have customers to serve. It's a catering tent, not a police interview room."

Nash ambled forward and collapsed on the juggler's feet. He groaned as Charlie used her bare toes to tickle him. He rolled over and presented his stomach to the room, all four legs waving in the air.

Lila sighed. "Geez, hound. Do you have any shame?"

"Little toes good," Nash grumbled and turned his head away, ignoring Lila.

"Give it up, kid. He can only see as far as the juggler's toes. You're trying to win a losing battle." Colin licked pink icing off a tiny cake. "Me? I see that tiny dame's got hidden depths. *Sneaky*. Like my goddess."

"No one's as sneaky as Elspeth." Xandie tapped short nails on the table. "Sofie lost it when she saw you. Why?"

Charlie gave Nash one more rub with her bare foot, then slipped her shoe back on with a sigh. "My family's complicated. Just ask Braun." She jabbed a finger at the police chief.

Zach shrugged. "We know all about Goldi Locks, but I prefer to judge a person's actions rather than their family history."

Xandie suppressed her cheer. She had to admit she kinda liked the perky juggler. Charlie reminded her of a combination of Elspeth and Miranda. A mixture of wicked-ness, snark, and potential danger. She had no doubt the juggler could defend herself. But was she capable of murder? "Did you kill my jeweler, Ernest Gem?"

Charlie leaned back in her chair. "The only time I saw Ernest Gem was when he snuck into the fair to have secret meetings with that sour-faced bear or that snooty silver-smith who thinks he's a goddess' gift to women."

Snooty Simon just kept popping up. Xandie switched gears. "Why did Sofie think you're after my ring?"

"Because my ancestor stole it from a fae smith, then she tried to steal from a Braun. There was a tussle and a Braun ended up dead, Goldie got arrested, and the ring got left behind."

Zach leant forward, frowning. "That doesn't explain my cousin's knee-jerk reaction to you."

"The Locks never met a job they couldn't finish, and they hold grudges." Charlie bit her lip. "They made it their mission to make the German Brauns' lives a misery. I don't think the rest of them realized the ring had even migrated to America."

"So, Sofie has a genuine grievance against your family?"

"Well, in my family's defense, which I can tell you hardly ever happens, the Black Forest Brauns have been killing any Locks they found through the decades."

"And this is all about the ring?" Xandie spread her hand flat on the table. The ugly, black discoloration had spread over the band and more spots were peeling.

Zach frowned when he saw the engagement ring. "It wasn't that bad when I gave it back to you, and the stone's missing now."

"The stone was super loose, so last night I gave it to the Library to look after. Then I shelved some books, and all the prongs that had held the stone snapped off. I was lucky I'd already rescued the stone." If she was brutally honest, she preferred the ugly peeling ring without the amber colored stone. Although earrings made from the stone might be nice.

"I'm not my family. If you do a background check, you'll see I've had nothing to do with them for years. But to answer your question, people want the ring, including the original owner, my family, and his whack a-doodle cousins." Charlie pointed to Zach. "Money and family feuds tend to make people do crazy things."

"Including murder and assault?" Xandie pressed.

"I'll cop to the assault, but not the murder. Besides, if you charge me with assault, you need to charge the pug. He helped."

"Hey. No narking on the pug." Colin shook his head, pink icing flying around the tent.

"Hey, watch it." Lila ducked behind the counter as icing flew.

"Can't keep a good pug down." He lumbered to his feet and stretched. "I was in the wrong spot at the right time. Besides, you have to catch me first, copper." The pug shot out of the tent as fast as his tiny legs could handle.

"A snail's faster than that snack-loving canine. Time to wrap it up, Braun. I got hangry customers. Arrest her or let her go."

Charlie held up her hands. "If it makes it easier, I'm the black sheep of the family. I ran away to the circus instead of thieving and carrying on the feud. I've since moved onto fairs, but they still hate me and won't have anything to do with me. I didn't murder the jeweler, but maybe you should be looking at the fair anyway."

"Thanks for the heads up, but..."

Xandie cut across her fiancé. "Who would you suggest we look at?"

"I've been at the fair for a while, and every time we pull into a new town, the same thing happens. Rough looking customers rock up, spend time with our silversmith, then disappear."

Zach shrugged. "Maybe they like jewelry?"

"The same customers all the time? Some are new, but most are repeat customers. And all transactions are conducted in the shadows." Charlie smiled sweetly. "I hate to tell you your job, but maybe look at the fair's past travel schedule and any unsolved murders or assaults." She winked at the police chief. "Just a suggestion, of course."

"I'll take your suggestion under consideration. You're free to go, Ms. Locks. But watch yourself. I don't care what feud our families have going on in other countries. Point Muse is my town, and I won't tolerate any mayhem."

"You tolerate Elspeth," Xandie pointed out fairly.

"That's different. It's not Point Muse without the wicked witch."

"Zach? Can I speak to you?" Matthew Grim, Point Muse's reaper and Lila's boyfriend, filled the catering tent entrance, his large shoulders blocking some of the morning sun.

"What now?"

Matthew cleared his throat. "Nothing. Just a feeling I'm getting from the crowd out here. Not what I'd expect from a small-town fun fair."

"See," Charlie said. "The fair's hinky. He's external corroboration."

"Do you need me to translate that word?" Xandie smiled at Lila, who just rolled her eyes.

"I don't care what external thing you have going on. Just take it outside." Lila flapped a hand, shooing everyone out.

Braun grabbed Matthew and drew him aside to speak in hushed tones.

"That's my hint to disappear into the crowd." Charlie waved to the cousins. "Don't stress, Librarian. I'll be lurking around, keeping an eye on you. No danger should come to your august presence." Charlie executed a perfectly elegant curtsey.

"Should we be concerned about Xandie?" Lila's snark dropped away, leaving only worry behind.

"The ring is at the center of all the mayhem. Who's wearing the ring?" Charlie paused, waiting for awareness to dawn. "Exactly. But like I said, I'll be around, and the Librarian's knife-happy mother is capable enough for close protection."

Close protection? "You sound like you know a bit about body guarding." Just who was Charlie Locks?

"I've been around. Learned a thing or two. Watch your back, Librarian." Charlie blew the women a kiss and disappeared out the back of the tent.

"Holly will be here any minute for her fortune teller shift. Between us and your man, we should have you covered." Lila twirled a curl of long brown hair around her finger. "You could take Nash. He likes you. He'll protect you."

"No feline," Nash growled from the floor where he still lay.

"The mouthy feline is back at the Library. He doesn't lower himself for fairs, apparently."

Nash shook himself and joined Xandie at the catering tent opening. "Okay. Going out."

"He's talkative today."

"He had cotton candy." Lila shuddered. "It doesn't agree with hellhound physiology. Can't shut him up now." She narrowed her gaze on her cousin. "I texted Holly. She's expecting you at her tent. No deviation from the planned route. Straight to Madame Hollita's tent. Got it?"

"I got it. I'm not Elspeth looking for chaos to feast on."

"We'll see."

Ignoring Lila, Xandie wandered toward the fortune teller's tent. A rumble of crowd noise, however, drew her toward the main tent where her mother had almost skewered her. A small crowd had gathered around a temporary workbench set up outside.

"If you move back, I will attempt to show you how to manipulate inexpensive jewelry wire into beautiful bracelets." Simon Wald glared at the crowd.

"If you'd turned up when the demonstration was supposed to start instead of arguing with that lady with the clipboard, you wouldn't be rushing now," an irate middle-aged woman yelled from the center of the crowd.

"That's it. I cannot work under these conditions." Simon slapped his jeweler's pouch closed and sneered at the crowd. "None of you appreciate fine art."

Way to rile the crowd. Point Muse was one town you didn't antagonize. They were used to dealing with the wicked witch and her mayhem. Who knew how they'd deal with the snooty jeweler? And why had he been arguing with Sabine? She was the only person Xandie knew at the fair who carried a clipboard. Xandie found it hard to imagine the organized Sabine getting upset enough to fight in public. Then again, Simon was a tax on anyone's patience.

"Go suck an egg," another woman yelled and threw a handful of cotton candy at the man. Or attempted to. In reality, it rained down on the crowd around her.

As if unlocking their inhibitions, a download of fair food pummeled the jeweler before the mob drifted away.

"I think Simon just lost his Point Muse fan-club," Xandie mumbled to her hellhound bodyguard. She watched as Simon packed up his makeshift working bench and stacked a few boxes, as well as a leather-bound book, on the top of the bench.

A man with long black hair and a hat pulled low over his forehead sidled up to the jeweler, and they had a hushed conversation.

Simon glared furtively around before grabbing the leather-bound book and scribbling in it, then he placed it back on the stack of boxes.

Xandie slid behind an arguing couple for cover as she watched the man with the black hair hand over a wrapped parcel to Simon. Making a snap decision, Xandie stepped out and strolled casually toward Simon, Nash at her heels. "That crowd wasn't too happy. Point Muse residents get snippy when their schedules are interrupted."

The tall, dark-haired man jerked and murmured something to Simon. The jeweler quickly handed over a small bag to the customer who immediately slunk away.

"Sorry, I didn't mean to chase a buyer away." Xandie smiled sweetly and leaned against the temporary bench, next to the pile of boxes and his mysterious ledger.

Simon sniffed. "If they are truly discerning customers, they will persist in their search for quality jewelry." He rested his hand on the leather-bound book for a moment before glaring at Xandie. "Have you found my missing jewelry yet? I have people who have ordered commissions. This will delay delivery."

"Was that what that man who you spoke to wanted? Some of your missing stock?"

Simon looked flustered for a moment. "The customer is ordering a bridal piece for his sister. A commission."

Xandie cocked her head, pretending interest. "I don't know how you do it. I can't remember anything, and you can memorize what he wanted and his details. Truly inspiring."

Clearing his throat, Simon tapped his book. "I have a ledger. Makes business more organized."

"Of course." Xandie nodded. "About your stock. Maybe you could provide a list of what's missing. Now, I'm not the police, so it's only a suggestion, and I'm only a Librarian."

"A nosy Librarian." Simon looked down at Xandie and fixated on her ring. "That is in an abominable state. I can clean and repair it. If you want."

Hecate-cursed ring. "There's an awful lot of people

interested in this piece of jewelry. Funny, since it looks so abominable."

"Quality adornment always creates an interest. Especially well-made pieces."

It was currently black and peeling. Xandie lifted a hand. "I don't know about well-made."

The jeweler's eyes sparked as outrage flashed across his features. "The artisan who crafted this piece had an exquisite talent. Unfortunately, it has fallen into uncaring hands, and that has caused this current predicament."

Mr. Jeweler sounded quite knowledgeable about a ring he'd only seen a few times. Xandie opened her mouth but was derailed by a furious Sabine, sweeping in with her ever present clipboard.

"Mr. Wald. We must speak about your food throwing debacle." Sabine stopped. "Ms. Meyers? I was under the impression you were at our fortune teller tent for your own protection?"

Nash grumbled low in his throat and pressed himself against Xandie's legs, pushing her back.

That's my cue to depart post-haste. "Heading there now. Thanks, Sabine, for reminding me." Xandie waved at the fuming fair administrator and scooted off in the direction of Holly's tent. She passed a huffing Melody Braun heading toward Simon and Sabine. The female bear shifter was on *Project-Stick-Close-To-Simon* in the hopes of some answers. Xandie heaved a sigh of relief as she reached Holly's tent unscathed. "No officious administrator can grump at me now. I'm doing exactly what I was told to." Xandie took a step into the darkened fortune teller tent. "I think someone's overdone the mood-lighting here. It's as dim as Hecate's boudoir." An old Elspeth saying referring to the Goddess of Magic, but it seemed appropriate.

Nash growled from the entrance, his eyes flickering red and the fur on his back standing on end. He grew in stature to the size of a small pony.

Xandie froze, elephants performing cartwheels in the base of her stomach. That was the hellhound's watch-out face. She took a sidestep and placed her body against the side of the tent, which still had a dark interior. *Darker than it should be.* This meant someone had likely hexed the interior into shadows. She shuffled to the side as Nash crowded in, his red eyes illuminating a glow around him.

"Nash?" Xandie hissed. "Are we safe? Can you..." Xandie stepped forward and her foot met something soft. She tried to scuttle away, but as she sidestepped, she collided with a chair. Xandie pitched forward and landed on her hands and knees. She reached out a hand and touched the rapidly cooling skin of someone stretched out on the ground.

Nash gave a sharp yip and burst into blue flames that wreathed his body and brightly illuminated the tent's interior. Including Xandie, sprawled on the ground, and Sofie Braun with a wire choker tightened around her neck... A very lifeless Sofie.

"Nash. We have a problem..."

THIRTEEN

"I am the victim here. Victim. Not suspect." Simon Wald slapped the interview table.

"You were late to your demonstration. Where were you?"

"That is what you're basing your suspicions on? I was speaking to the fair administrator. She delayed me. Talk to her."

Xandie adjusted the blanket her fiancé had given her after she stumbled across Sofie's lifeless body. "What was the disagreement about?"

Simon reared back, disdain written across his face. "Why is a Librarian interviewing me? Shouldn't that be law enforcement's job?"

Zach Braun shoved his shaggy sandy-colored hair back and sighed. "It cuts down on arguments. Just answer the questions, please."

"Anything to end this farce." Simon tapped his buffed nails on the police issue interview table. "That Sabine woman took umbrage to the fact my demonstration was unavoidably delayed. Of course, by talking to me, she delayed the start even more."

"And the original delay?" Xandie pushed. She was positive Sofie and Simon had a connection of some sort, even if the bear shifter had flirted with Zach. Plus, there was the murder weapon...a wire choker that matched the list of Simon's stolen stock he'd finally given to the police.

"A customer who wanted a private consultation. That side of my business is very lucrative and takes time to manage. That woman couldn't understand my reasoning." Simon's icy gray eyes slid sideways as he answered.

Shifty much? He definitely knew more than he said. "This customer? Is it one you've dealt with before?" Maybe the customer was the rough man she'd seen after the demonstration, handing over a packet to the jeweler. Money maybe? Just what was the attraction to snooty Simon's jewelry?

He shrugged. "Some customers prefer to come back to a quality they can depend on."

"And the fact the victim was found strangled by one of your metal chokers?" Zach interjected.

"Obviously, the killer and thief are one and the same." Simon settled back into his chair, smile firmly in place. "As I said, this has nothing to do with me."

"If your business is all aboveboard, then you won't mind showing us your records. That book I saw at your demonstration?" Xandie shot her own smile straight at Simon's smirking face. "The blue leather-bound one."

His smile dropped away. "This is persecution. I've done nothing wrong."

Xandie snorted. "Persecution? You think we have a deep-seated hatred of jewelers?"

Simon drew himself up. His glittering gray eyes flashed

with his ire. "I am part fae. This is because you hate us. I witnessed the fight you had with the representative of Lady Greenhand."

Disagreement maybe... Fight? Not on her slippery suspect's life. Xandie opened her mouth to rebuff, but Zach broke in.

"You're only half. The other's human. You were raised by your grandfather, who was a full fae. You spent time in Germany and England. Since my fiancée has only seen one fae and is human herself, I fail to see how your accusation of persecution has any merit."

The police chief stood and stared thoughtfully down at the jeweler. "I'm keeping you here for the next few hours while I check your alibi and look for your ledger. But I'll make sure you are released in enough time for the fair's special dinner tonight at Mayweather Inn. Perhaps you can speak to Mr. Greenhand about the disagreement with Ms. Meyers." Zach nodded to the frowning jeweler and tugged on Xandie's blanket.

"Ms. Meyers? Can you come with me for a moment?" He dragged Xandie outside the interview room, making sure the door was tightly closed behind them. "What happened to being seen but not heard?"

Xandie rolled her eyes. "You seriously bought that? Since when have I ever not talked? Besides, I thought my questions were good. Pointed."

"Except the fact you aren't law enforcement and he's not legally required to answer any of your questions." Zach bopped Xandie on the nose. "But yes, your questions were good. Can you please go home and get some sleep now?"

"Will you call me? Let me know what you find in Simon's van?"

"Yes. Now get." Zach pushed Xandie at a waiting Lila.

"Make sure she gets home safely and tuck her into bed, please." The bear shifter pointed a finger at the baker witch. "No side trips, got me, Lila Harrow?"

Lila held up a hand. "Don't get your fur in a tangle, chief. I solemnly swear on my grandmother's grave I will take Xandie straight home."

Following her cousin out of the station, Xandie stood next to Lila's decrepit, brightly painted bakery van. "Since when is Elspeth dead?"

"Well," Lila hedged. "She isn't, but if she was, I would definitely swear on her grave. I just figured you might have another destination in mind."

Xandie smiled slowly. "I love how devious Harrows are. And, in fact, I might have an idea or two."

Snooty Simon was a slippery character, and she had a feeling her fiancé might need some help... *An invisible helping hand.*

"Are you sure they've all gone?" Xandie peeked from behind a large bush at the edge of the parkland where the fair had been set up.

"Geez. What am I? A newbie?" Elspeth sneered at her granddaughter and pulled her black furry cap farther down over her head. Twin holes on each side of the cap allowed her dark blue pigtails to stick out.

"Did you really need to wear a wig tonight? No one can even see your hair."

"You're on my list, Lila. Watch your back." Elspeth snapped her fingers, and blue sparks flickered above her hand.

"Just a question." Lila lowered her voice. "She's in a mood. Did Colin have a tuna-related issue again?"

"Mathilde heckled her while she gave a hex demonstration at the fair. It didn't end well." Holly grimaced. "There may have been itching powder and indigo spots involved. The fair has banned both of them. Elspeth feels persecuted."

Even with one down, Black Forest bear shifters were menaces. Xandie had a thought. "What was Eric, Sofie's brother, doing while Mathilde courted a tragic itchy ending with Elspeth? I thought he'd be sticking close to the old bear now that Sofie isn't around. Solidarity in grief and all that."

Elspeth snorted. "Too busy binging on Lila's honey buns and watching back-to-back episodes of *Desperate Witch Wives*. I get the feeling there wasn't much love lost between those three."

"All this poop about family honor." Xandie curled her lip. "I think it's more what they can milk out of the bidders."

"Whatever the motivation, that old bear's going down." Elspeth cracked her knuckles and started to cackle.

Xandie slammed a hand over her grandmother's mouth. Weird things happened when Elspeth laughed. Not exactly covert when you're trying to break into a deserted fair. "No cackling. Remember the mission." She let her hands drift away from Elspeth.

Glaring, Elspeth made a production of wiping her mouth. "Fine. But you're on my list too. No one wants Librarian cooties. Who knows where or what that hand has shelved?"

"Can we focus?" Holly grimaced. "Do we all need to be here? I mean...isn't it overkill if we all search Simon's van for his little black book?"

"Scaredy banshee," Lila taunted. "It's just a little breaking and entering."

Punching her cousin in the arm, Holly pouted. "I just meant maybe there's something else one of us could be doing to maximize our skulking potential."

Elspeth smirked, teeth on show. "Why, little banshee. That's a great idea. You're our lookout. Let us know if anyone, up to and including the fuzz, comes along." The wicked witch dusted off her hands. "I love a good skulk. Let's get this show on the road." Elspeth hoisted her black jogging pants up and strode out from behind their bush.

"Hecate's gritted teeth." Lila lurched forward, dragging Xandie with her. "You know what she's like. Elspeth thinks she's the toughest witch on the block and can handle anything. So why bother checking to see if the coast is clear?"

"What am I supposed to do?" Holly whispered furiously.

Xandie winked at her cousin. "Hey, you wanted to do something different. You're the lookout. So, look out."

Lila snickered as she hauled Xandie toward the vans of the full-time fair employees.

"Don't you dare leave me out here by myself," Holly wailed and covered her mouth with her hand, looking frantically around.

"You'll be fine. Remember, you're a Harrow. Embrace the mayhem and make sure no one creeps up on us." Xandie gave her cousin a thumbs up. Poor Holly didn't leap into chaos like the rest of the family. The banshee witch liked to think things through, plus she really was more of a scaredy-cat than Xandie or Lila.

"That's Simon's van, right?" Elspeth pointed at a van that stood by itself a little way from the rest of them.

Xandie nodded. "That's the same van Charlie and I searched before. The police couldn't find the book. Apparently, Simon's claiming someone must've stolen it. All the fair employees have to go to a dinner at the inn tonight. It should be deserted here, at least for a little while."

"If they all had to go, why is Simon arguing with someone?" Lila pointed out. "Don't suppose you have an eavesdropping hex in your sneaky bag of curses and evil spells, Elspeth?"

The wicked witch wiggled into a spot next to the fortune teller tent and mumbled something under her breath.

"Excuse me? I couldn't hear you?" Lila pressed her grandmother.

Sighing, Elspeth spoke a little louder. "I'm having supply issues. Some hexes may be running low until I can get materials in to restock."

"What did you do this time?" The only time Elspeth ran out of stock was when she'd upset someone, and they refused to sell to her.

Elspeth inspected her fuchsia nails. "I may have cursed someone I shouldn't have with a shedding curse."

Xandie rolled her eyes. "In other words, you cursed your supplier's significant other to go bald. And they didn't appreciate it."

"Minor miscalculation."

"The other person could be Sabine, but I can't see clearly enough for a positive identification. Whoever it is, they're doing the finger point thing that Mom does to Elspeth." Lila frowned. "Simon has his arms crossed over his chest. So, he's feeling defensive, while the other person is aggressively pointing out his wrongdoings."

"Since when did you become an expert on body

language?" Xandie needed to read more non-supernatural books. Might help with sleuthing.

"I like watching witch soap operas. The foreign ones are the best. I like to guess what's going on."

"Uh-huh." The things you learned about family while on a skulking trip. "As per Lila's body language skills, Simon's annoyed. And the other person, possibly Sabine, is angry. Maybe she found out he's taking secret commissions and she's against it? That's why we need to get in and find his little book of customers. And it's a blue book, not black."

"Who cares? We ain't gonna get any kind of book by lollygagging here." Elspeth snapped her fingers in the other figures' direction. The shadowy person jerked as their phone rang.

Checking the screen of the phone before shoving Simon, the person dragged them both toward a parked car on the side of the road. A streetlight momentarily illuminated Sabine with a tight grip on Simon's arm.

"Who texted Sabine?"

Elspeth smirked at Xandie. "Just a heads up that Rose Mayweather's on the warpath about the fair employees."

"But she isn't. Won't Sabine be suspicious when she gets there and everything's fine?

"Please," Elspeth sneered. "That woman is always on the warpath. Something will set her off. How about we get sleuthing?"

Funnily enough, Xandie agreed with her grandmother for once, except for one thing... "Don't bother with Simon's van. Zach searched and couldn't find anything. We have to think out-of-the-box. Find somewhere else to search."

"If the fuzz can't find anything, why should we bother?"

"Xandie's already been through Simon's van once, then Zach. Makes sense to focus on another area. Why not let her choose?" Lila rolled her eyes. "Honestly, can't we just get on with it?"

"There are two areas we haven't looked. Simon's stall in the main tent and Sabine's van."

"Crack on then, Librarian." Elspeth waved Xandie into the lead.

"Main tent first." Xandie kept to the darker shadows and weaved her way through the different vans and stalls until they reached the big tent. "Simon's stall is at the back of the tent, on the far side." Even with the night's shadows, the moon above managed to glare down at the furtive group. *But inside the tent...* "Don't suppose you have any tricks to light our way, Elspeth?"

"I thought you'd never ask." The wicked witch of Point Muse reached into her jogging pants pocket and drew out a handful of little silver balls. Popping open the tent flap, she let the balls loose inside. They hovered for a moment in the air before exploding with a pop into tiny twinkling stars.

"I hate to compliment Elspeth, but that had style," Lila murmured to Xandie.

"Let's focus on the search. We have limited time before the fair employees return." Xandie headed straight to Simon's stall, her family trailing behind.

Lila smoothed a hand over the silver jewelry laid out on the top of the table. "For someone who's already missing stock, he's way too trusting. I wouldn't have left anything out overnight."

"Maybe this is stuff he doesn't care about as much?" Why was the other stock more important? Xandie crouched underneath the makeshift bench and searched through a stack of boxes piled haphazardly behind it. "Nothing weird here and no special blue book. Just parts for repairs and tools." She sat back on her haunches and grinned. "If we broke in for nothing, I'm going to be very disappointed."

"Breaking and entering is always good practice. And I wouldn't say it was for nothing." Elspeth held up a closed fist and slowly unfurled her fingers. Sitting in the center of her palm was a tiny empty vial.

"Okay, I'm missing the importance of an empty bottle." Obviously, it meant something to Elspeth and could be connected to any kind of devious mayhem.

"I need to test it, but only a few liquids come packaged that small in the hexing biz. And all of them cause mayhem and sometimes death. They aren't something a jeweler should have normal access to or any need to use."

"Unless the jeweler has a side business of something nefarious."

Elspeth just shoved the vial into her pocket and winked at Xandie. "Next sleuthing stop?"

No point in pushing for information from Elspeth. The old witch would divulge more details when she was ready. "Sabine's office then." Taking the lead, Xandie snuck to the tent's entrance and peeked out to make sure the coast was clear. "Sabine's office van isn't far away." Sliding between two vans, Xandie pulled up short next to a plain, nondescript van with Admin stenciled on the side.

Elspeth tapped a nail on the door handle, and a tiny blue spark flared for a moment before subsiding. The wicked witch grabbed the handle and opened the door with a flourish.

"That's much better than using Great-Aunt Rose's skeleton key," Lila said.

Xandie agreed with Lila. "Anything is better than using Rose's finger bone." She didn't bother to fight the shudder that rippled along her spine at the thought of the gray key.

"Can we speed the search up? I have a date with *Witch of Our Lives*. The witch channel's running a marathon."

And if Elspeth is occupied, it's a good night for all. Xandie stepped into the van and had a quick look around. Sabine's admin office was clean, tidy, and organized. Nothing personal or incriminating lay out in the open.

"This is a bust." Elspeth blew out a gusty breath. "The organization here gives me a rash." She scratched the back of her wrinkled hands and held them out to Lila. "See?"

"All I see is age spots."

"Why you..."

Xandie ignored her bickering family as she searched the tiny van. A small gray safe sat on the bench, door ajar. She rifled through the contents, but it only contained receipts.

"Let's get going. This place is too squeaky clean. We won't find anything here."

"There *has* to be something. Sabine seemed really angry at Simon, and Zach found nothing when he searched for the book. I'm sure there's something here."

"Have at it, girl. But I'm outie." Elspeth waggled her fingers and left.

"Elspeth has left the building...I mean the van. I repeat. Elspeth has left the van." Lila snickered at her own joke. "But she isn't wrong. I'll wait outside until you're done."

Waving at her cousin, Xandie focused. If Simon was doing underhanded, dodgy dealings at the carnival, surely Sabine knew? Or maybe she'd just found out. The administrator would have had time to hide Simon's evidence from the cops to protect the fair. And what was more likely, she would've hidden it somewhere close. That was probably why they'd been arguing earlier. Xandie ran a hand over the wall of the van. Everything seemed solid, no loose panels or hollow areas.

"There has to be something." She ran her eyes slowly over the van's interior. Everything in its place, organized, systematic. So, why did the couch look out of alignment? "For someone so organized, that should drive them crazy." Xandie considered the couch for a moment before sitting down. "Feels comfortable. Nice padding." She moved her bottom along the seat until she came to a firmer portion at the end of the couch. "That doesn't feel quite the same."

Jumping up, Xandie gripped the edge of the couch cushion, near the wall, and tugged it up. But it refused to move. Changing tactics, she grabbed the edge of the couch and tilted it slightly back toward her...exposing a small cavity below and a blue leather-bound book. *Simon's ledger.* "Bingo." Snatching out the book, Xandie let the couch's cushion slide back into place. She'd hit pay dirt.

Now let's see if snooty Simon's dodgy dealings equaled up to murder.

FOURTEEN

"He cautioned me for loitering. *Loitering.* He thought I was a creepy stalker," Holly raged.

"You were hanging outside a closed fair. I can understand why he gave you the warning."

"I was on lookout duty. You left me at the fair alone. It took me an hour to realize you'd left without me."

Xandie winced. "Elspeth left first, then I just wanted to get out with the book. Sorry." She patted Holly on the shoulder.

Lila choked back laughter. "Yep, sorry you are so forgettable. At least now you'll have a reputation for being a skulker. All of us must sacrifice for the sake of solving the mystery."

"I hate my family," Holly groaned and angled her head toward the table.

The solid thunk of bone on wood made Xandie grimace. She swiped a plate of Lila's pick-me-up apple slices and pushed them toward her cousin. "Try these. I think you need them more than we do."

Holly lifted her head and peeked through her bangs at

Xandie. "You remembered me enough to procure food. I am honored."

Lila slapped the back of her cousin's short, bobbed head. "I thought I was the drama llama, not you?"

"You do what you need to when you're labeled a skulker."

"Speaking of skulking and the reason behind it, did you find anything in that book you found?"

"Better be good if I was left skulking outside for hours," Holly growled.

"You're a skulker. Embrace your future." Lila settled a beady eye on Xandie. "But she has a point. Was anything worth risking jail time found in that book?"

"I spent most of last night going over it. Some of it is in code or a different language. I'm not sure which." Xandie lowered her voice as fair patrons wandered in and out of the catering tent. "Some of the orders are above board. But there are repeat names in the ledger and no sign of orders being filled. It's weird." With a quick glance around, Xandie opened her backpack and drew out a piece of paper with symbols and jumbled words scrawled across it. "I'm leaning toward a made-up language."

"It's fae. Some of the clans even have different dialects. They're tricky that way." Charlie Locks, perky fair employee, bounced up and down next to Xandie.

"Can you read it?"

Grimacing, Charlie twirled a strand of her curly wild blonde mop and considered the piece of paper Xandie held. "Maybe. Given time. Where did you get this from?"

"Ah, well. That is..." Xandie ground to a halt. What could she say? They'd broken in and stolen it from the fair?

Charlie tapped the paper. "Let me guess. You found snooty Simon's mythical ledger when the police couldn't?"

Xandie cleared her throat. "Depends on if you can read it or not."

"Gimme." Charlie waggled her fingers as Xandie held up a single piece of paper. "My fae is rusty, but the gist of it is an order for custom jewelry." Charlie frowned and read it silently.

"And?"

"Looks like from this partial transcription Simon was fencing dodgy jewelry for some rough customers. He also had a few special commissions, but all the book records are the locations, not who ordered them."

"Why not record names like he did for fencing his stolen goods then? Unless he's too scared to? Or..." Xandie puzzled over the enigma of Simon's secret ledger book.

"Or what?" Lila leaned in and rapped her cousin on the head. "Don't leave me in suspense."

"Unless he doesn't want to link a name to a location because what he gave them and what they did with it wasn't quite legal?"

Charlie snapped her fingers at Xandie. "Give the Librarian a prize. Tell me, did that brawny bear shifter of yours ever look at missing persons and unexplained deaths in the towns the fair visited?"

Why would... "I'm not sure, but I'm beginning to think it might be important." There was obviously more to Simon's side business than she'd first thought. Not to mention Charlie, the juggler, knew more than she let on.

"On that uplifting note, I need to disappear before Sabine accuses me of skulking. Cheers, witches." Snickering, Charlie slipped out of the tent.

"See what I mean? The whole skulking thing is going to follow me forever." Holly pouted and nibbled on one of Lila's apple slices. "These are good."

Lila bowed. "Why, thank you. Only the best for the catering tent and the fair."

"And the fair patrons thank you." Sabine bustled up, with her ever present clipboard in hand.

Xandie shoved her transcribed papers into her bag and straightened with a forced smile. "Sabine. Fancy seeing you here."

The administrator stared at Xandie, eyebrows arched. "Complete surprise for the fair administrator to be at the fair." She made a show of checking her clipboard. "I see your shift with the catering tent starts soon."

Lila stood. "She was having morning tea before starting her shift. Until then, Madame Hollita can help behind the counter. What don't you have a break, Sabine? You work so hard for the fair." Lila pushed Sabine into a chair next to Xandie and scuttled off behind the counter, Holly in tow.

"A few minutes wouldn't hurt, I guess." Sabine placed her clipboard on the table but kept it close at hand.

"Hopefully, the police searching Simon's van hasn't disrupted the schedule too much." Xandie slipped straight into interrogation mode. She caught Sabine's hands tightening slightly on her clipboard. A wary glint appeared in the administrator's eyes.

"Not really. The search was conducted outside of fair hours. There's no delay in timing currently."

"And, of course, the police found no trace of Simon's ledger."

"Mr. Wald may sometimes be unapproachable but, upon occasion, he can be a talented jeweler." Sabine offered Xandie a stiff smile, but her silver eyes drifted away before making eye contact.

"He definitely seems to be in demand. He has repeat customers who follow him from town to town."

"How did you know about his private customers?" Sabine's voice snapped out with force. She moderated her tone. "I mean, I'm sure some of his customers may choose to buy multiple items or come back again, but that's not the focus of his stall, of course."

Xandie nodded but kept her focus on the trickle of customers entering the catering tent as she puzzled out Sabine's words. On the surface, everything the administrator said made sense. But Xandie had a feeling the organized woman knew exactly what was going on at the fair. "Of course. Plus, the police searched but couldn't find Simon's ledger. They were obviously looking in the wrong spot."

Sabine shifted in a chair. "I have no knowledge of any ledger."

"That's what you told the police. But we know different, don't we?" Xandie turned her attention from the customers to the visibly nervous woman beside her.

"I have no clue what you mean."

"You don't? Surely you've seen Simon's little blue book? The one he writes his transaction details in? Well, the less than legal ones anyway. Pretty smart to write in an obscure fae dialect. Makes the information super private. Unless the reader understands the language, of course." Xandie beamed and drew out her transcribed papers. "Would you believe I found someone who understands this? Aren't I lucky?"

"Like I said, I have no knowledge of Mr. Wald's ledger."

Sabine's face could have been carved in stone. Xandie pushed a little more and went with her gut instinct. "Really? I'm surprised, since your name and a certain amount of money appear in the ledger weekly. In fact, I worked it out. I bet the amount paid to you is equal to ten percent of Simon's profits."

"I knew this would come back at me." Sabine sagged in her chair. "Could we keep our voices down?" She peered over her shoulder at the dining patrons. "I don't want this to get out."

Xandie complied and lowered her voice. "Talk to me, Sabine. Maybe I can help you."

Sabine groaned. "I should have stood my ground and said no, but the money..." She trailed off. "It's always greed that gets you, isn't it?"

"What happened?"

"This place has been running at a loss for years. The owners made me a deal. Turn a profit and the fair's mine." She shook her head. "I thought my organizational skills would turn the business around. Turns out no one likes fairs anymore. Especially not ours."

"Then Simon offered you a deal, I take it."

"Not at first, but our profit was so down, and his payoffs were just too good to refuse."

"When did you realize what he was really doing?"

"Do I look like an idiot? I knew from the beginning what he was doing wasn't legal. But I figured receiving and passing stolen goods was a minor charge. But then I snooped a little and found out it wasn't just stolen goods. He was making custom-made orders for certain customers. Repeat customers. I started watching the news and every time we arrived in town, the number of unexplained deaths rose."

The same thing Charlie had warned Braun to look for. The lights flickered on in Xandie's Librarian brain. "Simon had a side business of outfitting assassins."

"Or anyone who had a grudge and the right connections. When I realized, I tried to back out, but Simon threatened to tell the owners." Sabine fisted her hands on the table, white knuckles gleaming.

"You hid his ledger in your safe, knowing the police wouldn't look in your van."

Sabine nodded, then glared at Xandie. "Obviously, you didn't have the same set of ethics."

"I have no idea what you mean. Simon's ledger just happened to fall into my hands. "

"I heard about Harrows and Point Muse, but I didn't believe it." Sabine shook her head. "Simon talks about you and your ring all the time."

Ew. Creepy much? She'd barely even spoken to the jeweler.

Reading Xandie's discomfort, Sabine spoke quickly. "Not like that. He's obsessed with your engagement ring. Talking about antique heirlooms and how some families mistreat them without knowing their value. How it should go to its rightful owner or its original crafter, et cetera. Things like that."

How did he know the ring may have belonged to someone other than the Brauns? "Did he ever say where he got that information?"

"No. Just general rambling about the ring. I did see him meet that bear woman a few times at the fair. She seemed into him. If you know what I mean."

"Sofie Braun and Simon Wald?" Xandie shuddered. Not a power couple she'd have picked.

"They seemed intense when I saw them, but if you're thinking he killed her, you're wrong. He's not a killer. A blackmailing idiot, but not a killer."

"Somebody killed my jeweler and Sofie."

Sabine tapped her fingers on the tabletop. "I have no clue who. One of Simon's disgruntled customers maybe?

You have the ledger, so why don't you look through and find a likely suspect?"

"Maybe she's already looking at one." Elspeth strolled up, a lime green curly wig atop her head. She'd paired it with a hot pink jogging suit, matching combat boots, and a frilly, white lace apron tied around her waist.

Colin the pug trotted behind her with hot pink leg warmers on his tiny legs and a lacy white bib hanging around his neck.

"I am not involved in Simon's nefarious deeds or with any dead bodies." Sabine sneered at Elspeth. "I think your wig is too tight. It's constricting the blood flow to your brain."

Elspeth hissed.

Colin skidded to a stop and carefully sidestepped under a table.

Xandie gathered her gear and stood slowly so as not to spook the warring combatants. She had no urge to be in the line of fire.

"Why are you in the catering tent dressed like that? You're running the dunk tank. The catering shift this morning should be Ms. Meyers' task." Sabine glared at Xandie.

From contrite to cat in a second. Xandie was glad she didn't work at the fair permanently.

"I have minions to deal with the tank. I thought I'd help my favorite granddaughter nail a suspect to the wall and cook at the same time. Got a problem about that?" Elspeth pointed a glowing blue finger at the administrator.

"And you really wanted to taste the Devlin twins' black forest cake. You put on that apron and tried to wheedle your way into a taste test." Colin popped up for a moment. "My dame's got a powerful hunger for chocolate sponge, whipped cream, and cherries." The pug slipped back under the table.

Sabine stood and pushed her chair away. "Unless you are a paying customer of the catering tent, I suggest you get back to the dunk tank and leave the investigation to the police." She crossed her arms and glared at both Xandie and Elspeth. The noise of the tent rose sharply as multiple tables broke into coughing fits. Sabine glanced around, frowning.

"I think you should close your witch cake. You don't want to take me on, girly," Elspeth warned Sabine.

At the same time, someone at a table behind the wicked witch stumbled to his feet, weaving unsteadily, and collided with Elspeth.

"I'm threatening here. A little privacy please?"

"Sorry." The man lurched again, hand to mouth. "I don't feel so good." He bent over and retched on Elspeth's combat boots.

She shrieked and leaped back, just as multiple people stood, retching along with the man.

"Not again." Colin's voice slipped out from where he hid underneath the table.

"Again? This has happened before?" Sabine shrieked as a customer shoved her into a table as he ran out, heaving with spasms.

"There was a pet show and a few murders. I don't mean the sick people though," Xandie added hurriedly as more people bent over the table and chairs.

"This is all your fault." Sabine pointed at Elspeth. "There's no room in my schedule for food poisoning by disgruntled employees." She took a deep breath before shrieking, "You're fired. All the Harrows and Miss Snoop here as well. Fired and banned from the fair," Sabine added triumphantly.

Lila dumped a handful of napkins she carried onto the makeshift counter. "Thank Hecate's upset digestion. I'm so done with this fair." She dodged around vomiting patrons and grabbed Xandie's hand, dragging her to the exit. "Bonus is we don't have to deal with the black forest cake vomit cleanup."

Elspeth pointed two fingers at Sabine. "I'm watching you, Clipboard Girl." She shoved past her granddaughters with a flip of a long, green curl over her shoulder.

"Don't leave me here, my queen. Sick people and poisoned food are a pug's worst nightmare." Colin bolted from underneath the table, his pink leg warmer-covered legs scrabbling as fast as they could.

Like rats deserting a sinking ship, the Harrows departed the catering tent. But clipboard-obsessed Sabine wouldn't keep her away. Xandie had her number one suspect now, and like every Harrow before her, she was a dog with a bone when she had a sleuthing problem. Once she latched onto a target, she'd take it down.

Simon Wald's days are numbered...

FIFTEEN

"Banned? I've never been banned from anything in my life. I'm quiet. Bookish. I'm the good girl. This can't be happening to me." Xandie flung herself onto a threadbare, well-loved armchair in Harrow House.

"Welcome to the world of Harrow. We've been banned from most places." Holly counted off on her fingers. "Bubba's Bar and Grill, Fashions R Us, the laundromat, the dentist, Witchy Blooms, reading groups, the local witch coven. You name it, Elspeth's had us banned."

"I haven't even heard of those stores."

Lila joined the conversation. "Most of them closed down due to a series of not-publicly-connected-to-Elspeth-Harrow incidents."

"Elspeth Harrow incidents?"

Holly nodded. "No evidence linking Elspeth to pipes breaking or freezing over, rats, mice or any kind of rodent infestation, power outages or surges, or food rotting. Deny. Deny. Deny."

"That part I recognize. Isn't that our family motto? Deny. Deny. Deny?"

"Never get caught, and if you do, deny, deny, deny. You should know that, Xandie dear." Winifred Harrow swept in with a plate of cookies. "I'm trying a new recipe. Maple syrup cookies. See what you think." She placed the cookies in the middle of a small coffee table and stepped back as the cousins swarmed the plate of sugary treats.

"Thank Hecate's sweet tooth Lila didn't cook these," Holly mumbled around a full mouth.

"I'd take offense, but we all know my baking kryptonite is cookies. These are yummy though." Lila grabbed two cookies, one for each hand, and retreated.

Following her cousin, Xandie grabbed two and moaned her delight as she nibbled around the edge of a cookie.

"Oh, good. I'll keep that recipe then." Winifred beamed at the girls. "Nice to have someone appreciate your work."

"No one appreciates mine." Elspeth stomped in wearing pale rose-colored combat boots, matching flamingo pink jogging suit, and a migraine-inducing neon pink mohawk. She slumped into a chair, her skinny legs spread wide and a pouty look on her face.

"Who stole your candy, dark witch?" Lila took a large bite of her remaining cookie. "Do calories count when you've just been banned from the fair?"

"No, Lila. Calories never count when you've been banned from paid entertainment," Holly deadpanned before ruining the effect with a little snicker.

"Get back on topic. *Me.*" Elspeth thumped her bony chest. "Because of your antics, I'm banned. What have I said about getting caught?"

"Firstly, you hated that tank since Mathilde dumped you. And, secondly, we didn't cause the issue in the catering tent." Xandie crossed her arms and glared at her grandmother, cookie forgotten.

"A hex bag under the counter caused the issue in the catering tent." Elspeth sniffed. "Not up to my standards, but I guess witches can't be choosers."

"Give up the guilt, old woman. You know it wasn't us. Otherwise, you'd be on the warpath about restoring Harrow honor because we got caught. Since you aren't, that means you know we didn't cause the nausea." Lila blew on her short nails and buffed them on her shirt. "It ain't rocket science."

Silence reigned in the Harrow House sitting room. Everyone stared wide-eyed at Elspeth, waiting to see her reaction.

Frowning, Elspeth kicked her combat boots off the floor a few times before rolling her eyes at her family's antics. "Relax, you all. I'm not going on a rampage. The baker's right. The bunch of you are thicker than two Witchshine barrels, but that still makes you smarter than most of Point Muse."

"The killer's setting us up. Trying to discredit us." Xandie paced the floor and held up the peeling, tarnished ring. "A little thing to cause such drama. I guess there's no accounting for taste." Whatever the jeweler had done to the ring, patches had now peeled off, exposing the silver-edged flower designs in sporadic areas around the band.

"The killer knows you're closing in on them and using this to distract us and make sure no one believes you when you finally accuse someone?" Winifred wrung her hands. "I think this requires more baking. Baking helps me cope with stress." Xandie's aunt snatched up the empty cookie plate and hustled out.

"She'll be fine. Sleuthing always stresses her out." Holly dusted off her hands and sat up straight, clearing her throat.

"My bosses have a preliminary finding on Sofie's cause of death."

The Elysian Fields Funeral Home owners, and her bosses, Hector and Hillary, used their twin necromantic and funeral home expertise to help Point Muse law enforcement...*sometimes*. "What did your bosses find out?"

"Remember, this is only preliminary," Holly cautioned, her eyes gleaming.

"Yeah." Elspeth waved off the warning. "Spit it out, Death Girl."

"Sofie was strangled." Holly paused dramatically, waiting for her family's reaction. Her face fell as everyone seemed underwhelmed with the news. "You're all so jaded. Sofie was strangled by a silver choker. She also had contusions on the back of the head. Probably from falling to the ground, and she had bruises on her back, possibly from a knee."

"It's obvious she was strangled. When I found her, the choker was wrapped around her neck." Xandie offered an encouraging smile with her words. Like all Harrows, the witches weren't happy unless they were the center of attention. Out of all the cousins, Holly was the quietest, and less of a drama llama than Lila or Xandie, but an odd word of encouragement wouldn't hurt.

"Well, the choker matches one of Simon Wald's missing jewelry pieces. Hector had a good look at the choker and found some anomalies in the design."

"Wahoo. I like anomalies. Continue, favorite granddaughter."

"Favorite? That's what you told *me* when I brought you my orange cakes," Lila protested, her bottom lip pouty.

Elspeth shrugged. "It changes. Time is fluid. Continue, banshee."

"Don't steal my moment." Holly glared at Lila before continuing. "There are some interesting modifications to the choker that aren't standard."

"How unusual could an ornate silver choker be? What's standard?"

"At the center of the choker is a thick, circular disc with decorations etched into it. From there, on each side, is a decorated metal tube. At each end of the tube is some sort of metal spacer, then a chain is connected to that. It latches at the back of the neck snugly."

"Sounds like a normal choker." Lila shrugged. "Not impressed, banshee."

"The whoopie is what Hector found when he detached the choker from the dead bear shifter. The center disc has silver wire wound inside it. You pull the excess wire out by the spacers at the end of the tube. Someone put the choker around Sofie's neck, grabbed each side of the tube, pulled the spacers, and the wire slid out and choked her. They dropped her onto the ground when they were done. The choker is a deliberate weapon for killing." Holly sat back, a satisfied smile on her face.

"Simon's jewelry doubles as weapons of assassination. No wonder Charlie told us to look at the number of missing person deaths in the area that the fair visited."

"And?" Lila encouraged Xandie.

"And old snooty Simon is running a covert weapons supply business out of the fair. I bet a large proportion of his custom ordered jewelry is covert assassination weapons. No wonder he hid his ledger." *The ledger.* Xandie spun and pointed to her grandmother. "You wanted to look at the ledger after we were banned from the tent this morning. Where did you put it?"

Elspeth snorted. "That was hours ago, girl. I'm old. How am I supposed to remember? My memory comes and goes."

Holly snorted. "You have the memory of an elephant. More likely, you want to make sure your name doesn't appear in his ledger before you give it back to us."

"That's not the question you should be asking. There's one everyone's missed." Elspeth beamed, white teeth on show. "The question is, how did Little Miss Perky know about snooty Simon's weapons business? And FYI, the ledger is in my creation cave, and my name does not appear to be mentioned."

"You think that Charlie has something to do with Simon's dodgy business or something to do with Ernest and Sofie's murders?" Charlie, the perky juggler, was annoying, but Xandie wouldn't have guessed her for a murderer. At least not without just cause.

"Oh, that girl's as underhanded as they come. She's definitely up to nefarious deeds. I wonder if she's related to us?" Elspeth pondered.

"Whatever Charlie's up to, it doesn't matter. Simon Wald's our killer. I'm positive. But what's his angle? Anyone who's been interested in the ring has died so far. Why does he want it?"

Elspeth winked at Xandie. "Not everyone interested is dead. That fae from Mayweather Inn is still alive and kicking, and so is good old Simon."

"*About Simon.* Hillary told me he's gone missing. Braun's deputies are looking, but he disappeared after he was released from questioning."

"We saw him at the fair the night he was questioned, and then he was supposed to do that fair employee dinner.

So, either between the fair and then the inn, or after the dinner, he disappeared."

Lila nodded at Xandie's words. "But was it voluntary or is he another victim?"

Xandie opened her mouth to reply, but a thunderous knocking on the door distracted her. "Hold that thought until I shoo away our visitor." She stomped toward the door, nibbling on a short nail. She was positive Simon was the villain, but she had to prove it somehow. Xandie flung the door open, surprising Charlie Locks practicing a handstand on the front porch. "Doesn't that give you a headache, being upside down?"

Flipping right side up, Charlie smoothed her perky blonde ponytail. "Nope. I find it helps me think."

Perky should be outlawed. Especially in the middle of a murder investigation. "What can I do for you, Charlie?"

Charlie wedged her foot in the door. "Not what you can do for me but what I can do for you...yada, yada, yada."

"And?" Xandie pushed Miss Perky for an explanation.

Charlie strolled into the hallway. "Wow, this place is really old. You can just feel all the Harrows before you." She placed a hand on the wood-paneled wall. "Thanks for letting me in. Appreciate it."

The wall rippled under Charlie's hand before she snatched it away. "Whoa. That's something to get used to. I'd heard Harrow House was different. But this is awesome." She spun and clapped her hands. "This would be a perfect place for a party."

Xandie snorted. "Tried that recently with a karaoke party. Didn't turn out great." She led the way into the sitting room.

"I heard about the food fight. Seriously epic party."

"I'm glad someone appreciates my awesomeness." Elspeth pointed at the bubbly woman next to Xandie. "I like you. The perky acts are a bit much, but your capacity for chaos makes you interesting."

Charlie curtsied. "Thank you, wicked witch. That's a compliment coming from you."

"At least it wasn't a curse," Holly muttered and then coughed as her mother whacked her on the back of the head.

"Manners. We have a guest. Try and be less of a Harrow." Winifred beamed at Charlie. "Grab some snacks. I just baked."

Bouncing into a comfortable chair, Charlie arranged herself and crossed her legs. "Right. I'm ready."

Can a perky overdose affect brain function? "What for?"

"Your questions, Librarian. Theories, interrogation. I'm ready, so go for it." Charlie uncrossed her legs, and one started bouncing up and down.

"Are you high on Witchshine?" Lila blurted out bluntly.

"My mouthy cousin means no offense. Perky doesn't do well in Harrow House. Or with any Harrow, anywhere," Holly added.

"Sorry. Force of habit. It's a requirement for fair work." Charlie stilled her fidgety leg. "I thought you might want me to translate that ledger."

Definitely a good idea, but Xandie had a feeling Charlie had prepared a whole monologue if anyone had any questions for her. First question was how did she know about the missing people and unexplained deaths in the fair's locations? "You know what? That would be great. I'm sure our police chief will value your input if it leads to a break in the case."

"Yep. That's definitely why I did it." Charlie winked at the Harrows.

"The book's in Elspeth's creation cave, out back. When we're finished talking, we can take you out there, and you can have a look. See what you think."

"I'll get on translating it straight away. The last day of the fair is tomorrow, so I'll have more time after that."

"Not much time to catch a killer before the fair moves on."

A smile twitched the corner of Charlie's mouth. "About that. Due to Simon going missing, and the fact there are two outstanding murders connected to the fair, the very beary police chief has ordered the fair to remain in town until Simon's found."

Xandie glanced over at Elspeth to find a shrewd, calculating look on her grandmother's face. She had a feeling the wicked witch of the Harrow clan didn't believe Charlie's act either. Even now, sitting in the relatively safe Harrow House, Charlie looked like she'd spring into action in a heartbeat if something happened. Just like Xandie's mother, Miranda... *The black ops' agent.* Maybe it was time for interrogating. "How did you know about the missing people? Simon's side business? Why did you tell me to pass it on to my fiancé?" Xandie arched her brow. "Don't tell me you're just observant because I've seen your level of awareness before from a government agent. Who are you?"

Charlie smiled slowly without the manic edge that normally accompanied it. "I was warned about the Harrows. You're all quite entertaining. No wonder you're so sought-after."

"You're talking about my mother's black ops adventures and Elspeth working for the government during World War Two?"

Elspeth broke in. "I call those the dark days when my brain went AWOL."

"And those occasional buying trips you go on for your hex materials." Charlie smiled wide.

Every muscle in Elspeth's body stiffened. Shadows in the darkening room thickened around the wicked witch. "Aren't you the interesting one with all sorts of information?"

"You work for the government." Just like Xandie's mother and apparently, Elspeth, upon occasion.

"I work for someone who's concerned at the high number of casualties appearing after Simon Wald sells his custom jewelry. My employer is very motivated and would like the problem resolved without any more casualties. I'm here to offer any help I can. We'll have fun." She clapped her hands and smirked at the room.

"Great. Another spook in Harrow house." Lila leaned back in a chair, disgusted. She pointed a finger at her grandmother. "And don't think we'll forget about your government-funded buying trips. You got some explaining to do, Elspeth 'I-hate-the-fuzz' Harrow."

"We'll discuss this later. Right now, let's talk about perky in disguise." Elspeth hurriedly tried to distract her family.

Holly nodded. "For once, Her Witchiness is right. We need a plan of attack. A thorough plan that we do not deviate from, and no one ends up in danger...*again*." Holly glared at Xandie. "We both know what always happens. One of us ends up tied in knots. Literally."

"I do have a plan. But I need to talk to Tyr Greenhand at the inn tomorrow. I figure if I head out at lunchtime, after eating so much of Rose's heavy food, he won't run away from me."

Lila tapped a foot on the ground. "What's next after that?"

Xandie would have replied but the lights flickered overhead and the floorboards under her feet rattled, sidetracking her reply.

"What now?"

SIXTEEN

"House? You okay?" Harrow House had become sentient after putting up with generations of Harrow witches. Sometimes the house got moody and playful and moved stairs and walls to confuddle its residents. The windows in the sitting area rattled loudly in response to Xandie's query.

"That doesn't sound good." Xandie jumped up and peered out the rattling window. Night had begun to fall and coated Harrow land in shadows. Out of the corner of the window, Xandie could just make out the edge of Elspeth's creation cave, a.k.a. her Witchshine shed *and* home of Simon's nefarious ledger, as well as a large shadow that scuttled around its corner. "We have a problem."

Another shadowy figure stepped out from the tree line at the same time. Xandie squinted but couldn't quite make out any features. Maybe Simon Wald had decided to visit?

A loud slam sounded at the back of the house, and the echo of multiple paws hitting the floorboards in a rhythmic pattern heralded the arrival of Colin and Lila's hellhound, Nash.

Colin skidded into the sitting room. "Buckle up, witches. We got incoming."

Nash towered over the pug, his eyes lit with red flares. "Protect pet."

Lila groaned. "How many times do I have to tell you? You're the pet. Not me."

Elspeth stood and stretched, cracking her knuckles. "About time we had some action. Lack of mayhem makes my bones ache."

Winifred appeared in the doorway, wringing her hands. "There's something in the back yard. The dogs spotted it."

Charlie stood. "I'm happy to help in any way I can."

Xandie nodded. "I think I saw someone in the tree line at the front of the house. It looked like a man, but I couldn't identify who it was."

Nodding, Charlie headed straight for the front door. All perkiness dissipated in the face of immediate threat. "I'll take them on out front. Protect your back, Librarian. A lot of people are watching how you handle certain areas. Impress the right people, and who knows what might happen?"

"I could care less. This is about protecting the family." Xandie nodded to the not so perky secret agent and turned to Elspeth. "That's settled. Now, let's go kick some killer patootie."

"You heard it, girls. We have the Librarian's permission. Harrow witches, let's go cause chaos." The cackling wicked witch of Point Muse spun and headed for the back porch with her granddaughters and four-legged minions following. Flinging the back door open, Elspeth strode onto the porch and stood with hands on hips, surveying the shadowed yard. "Whoever you are, you're on Harrow land. Be prepared to defend yourself."

"She sounds like a pirate ready to board and raid their witch victims," Lila whispered to Xandie.

Winifred cleared her throat. "I'll stay here and protect the back door in case you need to retreat."

"I'll guard the door too. From the inside. With the door closed." Holly slid in next to her mother. "No matter what, we'll keep the door free of invaders. Get out there and kick butt, Harrows." Holly pulled back inside and slammed the door shut. She gave the women a thumbs up through the glass panel of the door.

"Oh, she's a brave one." Lila snorted, then straightened. "That old witch isn't the only one who can mix it up. Let's go, Librarian."

"Yeah, except we aren't wicked witches. You bake and I shelve books." Xandie stepped off the porch and grabbed a large branch that had fallen off a creepy old tree.

"I have my own secret weapons." Lila grabbed Colin as he trotted past and hoisted him on her hip. "Knowing Colin, he's probably already eaten something he shouldn't have. He's locked and loaded. Intruders beware."

"Yo, doll face. Could you let me loose? It ain't so fragrant under here."

"Shut it, secret weapon." Lila bopped the pug on his nose. "No insults, thanks. Just be ready to let loose if we find trouble."

"This won't end well," Xandie muttered but held up her branch. A skittering noise to the left had her spinning, but only shadows greeted her. "Where's Elspeth? She's too quiet."

Nash padded a few meters in front of them, his eyes flaming red and lighting a path. He pulled up next to the side of the house, not too far away from Elspeth's creation cave, body tense.

Creeping up next to Nash, Xandie paused when she spotted Elspeth at the edge of Nash's red glow. Their grandmother stood glaring at the open door of her Witchshine shed.

"Get your stinking shadow out of my shed," Elspeth roared.

"So much for the element of surprise." Her grandmother didn't have a subtle bone in her body. Xandie glanced toward the tree line at the front of the property and watched as Charlie threw herself at the shadowy male figure, taking him down. They fell to the ground with Charlie ending up on top. She began slamming her fist into her attacker's face. Looked like the perky juggler/government agent could handle herself. Xandie stepped up to Elspeth, branch at the ready. "Have you seen anything yet?"

"Short, hulking, spider shaped. Metallic. That's all. But if it doesn't get out of my shed, it'll be a flat pancake."

The only warning Xandie had was a tightening on her finger of the Braun family heirloom. At the same time, a large, metallic spider scuttled out of the shed and headed straight toward Xandie and Elspeth.

Elspeth yanked a small green bag out of her pocket and flung it at the creature with a blood curdling scream.

Frozen for a moment, Xandie wasn't prepared when Nash bounded forward, smoke trailing out of his nose as he rushed past and bumped into Xandie, knocking her over. Xandie dropped her branch as she hit the ground.

Lila placed Colin next to her and snatched up her cousin's branch, advancing next to Elspeth, whose green bombs had lit up the area and the creature.

"What in Hecate's blue barnacles is that?"

"You know, kid? I don't rightly know, but this little pug

ain't built to take on metal spiders. I'm outta here." Colin turned tail and headed for the back porch.

For once, the mouthy minion was right. None of them were up to dealing with the creature in front of them. Made of silver metal, copper wires, and other assorted metal pieces, the creature closely resembled a small, pony-sized, metal spider. Not something a Librarian with a side job of sleuthing regularly encountered.

Nash lunged forward, grabbed onto a spider leg, and tugged. A high-pitched squeal emanated from the metal intruder.

Elspeth screeched and threw herself over its back, jamming a small hessian bag in one of its metal panels. Smoke poured out from underneath the spider, and the mechanical monster lurched to one side. Elspeth slid from side to side, yodeling as if she were a rodeo rider.

Xandie winced as the spider bucked Elspeth off, still yodeling as she hit the ground. Xandie's ring tightened on her finger again, and she attempted to scramble to her feet. The last time the ring had squeezed her finger, a rabid metal spider launched itself at her.

A pinch on her ankle followed by hissing noises froze Xandie. Still on her hands and knees, she swung her head around and stared into a Frankenstein mishmash of metal in the shape of a large dog, with a hessian bag hanging off its neck, and a book-sized shape within. *Simon's ledger*. Xandie yelled and kicked out, but the metal canine latched onto her ankle again and dragged her back a few paces.

Flat on her stomach, Xandie scrambled as the metal intruder dragged her bit by agonizing bit away from the others. The spider had obviously been a distraction. Simon wanted his ledger back. The dog released Xandie's foot, and instead, lunged at her hand, nipping the air over Braun's engagement ring. Obviously, the ledger wasn't the only thing Simon wanted.

"A little help here?" Xandie bellowed and kicked out at the dog as it tried to bite her hand and take the ring.

"Be right witch you." Elspeth cackled and flung herself at the spider, blue electricity wreathing her fingers and hands. "I'm just gonna show this metal arachnid who's the boss."

"Always with the mayhem. How about a little divine help? Hecate, you around for an assist?" Nothing, nada. No help coming. She'd have to get herself out of trouble before metal Cujo fed on her finger. Speaking of a finger... She waggled the hand that had the ring. "How about you give me some help, please?" The ground surged under Xandie, heaving her up and down. She squeaked and held on, her fingers digging into the dirt.

The metal dog lunged forward, attempting another run at the ring, but stopped with a metal clang that sounded suspiciously like a yip of pain. It tried to yank itself forward but instead, toppled to one side. Large green vines clamped around its legs, squeezing until jarring pops sounded as one of them detached. It fell uselessly to the ground. The vines quivered again before covering the metal dog completely. Only the bag with the stolen book was visible. The vine covered the metal mound, but the dog shuddered and surged off the ground, before falling back to finally lay still.

The vines receded and disappeared into the dirt, leaving the shattered remnants of the metal dog behind.

Xandie expelled a gusty sigh of relief. Her ring had saved the day and nature had kicked science and magic's butt.

Charlie wandered up. Her hand covered a large

bleeding gash on her forehead. "Looks like it's Harrow-one, invaders-zero."

"Did you get the shadow guy? Was it Simon?"

"Whoever it was had a concealment hex over their face. But the build was Simon Wald's. He sucker-punched me with a rock and managed to bolt." She grimaced. "I must be losing my touch. How humiliating."

Xandie managed a smile at the woman's disgust.

"I'm ready and armed. Let me at them." Holly stood panting, eyes wide and a solid wooden rolling pin clasped in her shaking hands.

"Settle down, Xena, Warrior Princess. By the looks of it, Xandie rescued herself."

"Actually, it was the ring." Suddenly, Braun's family heirloom seemed kind of cool. *Shame someone was ready to kill for it...*

SEVENTEEN

"I don't think this is a good idea." Xandie grimaced as she slid off Elspeth's hot pink moped. She winced as she settled on her feet. A good night's sleep hadn't been long enough to stretch out her abused muscles from last night's metal monster attack.

Elspeth shook her long, raven-black, curly wig as she removed her helmet. "Your plan. You wanted to warn that fae he might be in danger. If it were my plan, hexes and my enemies squawking like chickens would be involved."

Xandie shuddered and shoved Elspeth's spare helmet back at her grandmother. Elspeth wasn't one for compassionate warnings. The wicked witch of Point Muse was more likely to be storming the inn rather than rescuing one solitary fae. "Two people are dead because they wanted the ring. I can't let there be a third if I have a chance to stop it."

"Bleeding heart. You get that from your grandfather." Elspeth sneered and parked her moped in a small garden next to the inn's porch.

Rose Mayweather will not be impressed. Xandie cleared her throat. "I'm pretty sure that isn't a parking space."

"That old love goddess wannabe shouldn't plant her garden so close to the front porch. I'm old. I need to get as close to the stairs as possible." Elspeth stomped onto the porch, raven hair swinging madly and dark purple sneakers silent as she trod the weathered boards of Mayweather Inn.

This time, Xandie's grandmother had matched her black hair and purple footwear with a light lilac jogging suit. Xandie made a note to ask her grandmother where she bought her outfits as it seemed like she had a never-ending supply of brightly colored jogging suits. It had to be magic or a very smart marketing ploy.

"Don't bring your feud to my establishment, Elspeth Harrow. You hear me?" Rose Mayweather stood in the doorway, hands on the hips of her fifties style, frothy petticoat dress. Rose's gray-blonde hair lay contained in a haphazard, messy bun.

"I promise Elspeth isn't here because of mayhem." Xandie corrected herself. "Well, *I'm* not here to cause any drama. We just need to speak to that fae who's staying here."

"Tyr Greenhand? That pompous man is taking his lunch in a private corner of my dining room." She snorted. "Like any part of Point Muse is private. It's a small town. Everyone knows each other's business." She held the door open but paused to glare over Elspeth's shoulder. "That poisonous pug with you, is he? I can't afford to have him clear my head out just because he had one too many lobsters."

Elspeth drew herself up to her five-foot-nothing height, eyes flashing. "No one maligns my pug. You shouldn't make fun of someone's delicate condition. Makes you a bully, Rose Mayweather." The wicked witch of Point Muse swept past the open-mouthed inn owner and swung through the dining room doors.

"But... I..." Rose closed her mouth and glared at Xandie.

"Hey. Don't glare at me. You know how she is about the pug. Best not to say anything and deal with the fallout later. Not that there will be any fallout," Xandie babbled as she slid past Rose. She offered a weak smile. "I'll try and minimize the damage."

Xandie stepped into the dining room and breathed a sigh of relief. Elspeth stood calmly to the side of the booth where the fae sat. No other calamity had descended. No floods, no fire or mayhem. Maybe Elspeth had turned over a new leaf.

"You're a Greenhand. Does that mean you're freeloading off a distant relative? Isn't that how you people do things?"

No new leaf, just a mouthy wicked witch. Xandie rushed to fill the conversational hole that Elspeth had dumped them into. "No offense. This is her nice behavior." She shot a narrowed glance at a smirking Elspeth.

"Elspeth Harrow's reputation precedes her, and I was briefed before the mission." Tyr Greenhand carefully wiped his mouth with a snowy white napkin and deliberately placed it next to his barely touched lunch.

"Scoot over, old man. My legs need a rest." Elspeth dropped into the booth seat and scooted closer to the man who'd plastered himself against the edge of the bench seat in horror. "What mission are you blathering on about?"

Tyr gathered himself and smoothed his long silver hair, restoring his composure. "The Librarian's ring belongs to my Lady Greenhand. We have tried to track its progress for generations but had no luck until it resurfaced here, in Point Muse, on *her* finger." He pointed to Xandie's tarnished ring.

Xandie slipped into the booth opposite her grandmother. "That's why we're here. Two people interested in this ring have been murdered. We wanted to warn you since you're interested in it as well."

Tyr raised a narrow-arched silver brow. His eyes glittered like hard emeralds. "How altruistic of you."

"It's the do-gooder gene she inherited from her grandfather. It drowned out my mayhem DNA. It's a constant disappointment for me."

Xandie ignored her mouthy grandmother. "Someone's removing the ring's competition. I wanted to warn you, so you can keep an eye out."

He nodded. "Worthy aspiration, but I am fae. No one will take me unawares."

And the man obviously possessed a colossal ego as well. Handy when one was intelligence gathering. "Of course. But I'm new to my position and know so little about the fae." Xandie smiled sweetly and ignored Elspeth's muffled snort. "Especially one so important that he was sent on a secret mission."

Tyr puffed out his chest. "Naturally. But it's impressive you can see your ignorance and seek to enlighten yourself. Commendable for a witch and a human."

"Why you..." Elspeth spluttered.

Xandie continued, "You're a special envoy to Lady Rosalind Greenhand?"

"I am an equerry to milady. A vassal of the family Greenhand, and I have the honor of possessing the same bloodline."

"Impressive." Xandie tapped the ring. "Almost as impressive as this jewelry. Did you know it defended me and tore apart a metal spider the killer sent to take the ring last night?"

The fae's supercilious expression dropped away, revealing a sharp cunning. "Someone tried to take the ring and it defended you?"

"Yes."

Tyr sat back and tapped his fingers on the table, a considering look upon his face. "Interesting. The ring has never worked for anyone else, but then milady has never so much as glanced at the ring as it was stolen before it was to be delivered to her."

"Greenhand? That means nature-based gifts, correct?"

"What makes you say that, Librarian?"

Xandie held up her ring hand. "Because vines from under the ground squashed the metal spider into pieces. With the name of Greenhand, combined with a magic ring that has roses etched on it, it's a solid assumption."

"Hmm." Tyr sat back, staring at the ring Xandie still held in the air. "The Greenhands have an affinity with the land. We cannot work metal such as that which attacked you."

Now they were getting somewhere. Xandie lowered her hand and toyed with the ring. "Can other faes work with metal?"

"Most don't, although a few clans have made a name doing so."

"Any clans that have the ability to make murderous metal spiders and nasty metal dogs?"

Tyr pursed his lips. "A name springs to mind."

"Care to share?"

"Schwartzwald. A fae metal smith clan from the Black Forest."

"Black Forest?" The same place the Brauns originated from? *What a coincidence.*

"Indeed. Albert Schwartzwald was a highly esteemed

metal worker. A large number of fae clans sent their commissions to him and his son."

"Including Lady Rosalind?"

Tyr inclined his head. "Unfortunately, the smith allowed milady's commission to fall into the hands of a blood-thirsty thief."

"Goldi Locks." Charlie's great, however many greats, grandmother.

"Then it fell to the bear shifter clan and disappeared until now." He nodded at Xandie's ring.

"What happened to the metal smith?" If anyone would have a motive, it would be the original crafter of the ring.

"He was shunned, of course." Tyr looked surprised that Xandie would even ask. "He failed to protect his commission. Honor has been tarnished. There are consequences."

Xandie sighed and blew a frizzy brown curl out of her eyes. "Let me guess. The only way to restore his family honor is to return the ring to Lady Rosalind before anyone else does."

"Albert Schwartzwald and his clan are a very old family. The clan knew the risks of not delivering."

Elspeth yawned. "How interesting... Not. Can we get to the good stuff before I die of old age?"

"Where is Schwartzwald now?" Xandie reminded herself not to take her grandmother on her next interrogation.

"Residing in England, I believe. His son and human daughter-in-law died suddenly in an accident involving some Germani. He raised his two grandchildren in England after the accident."

A combination of fae and human genetics, an English accent, and an ability to work metal meant Simon Wald was probably the grandson of the ring's creator. No wonder he wanted that ring. He wanted to restore his grandfather's honor and was willing to kill to achieve it.

"What does Germani mean? Not that I'm really interested. I'm just passing the time until I can hex someone." Elspeth winked at the fae as he tried to shift farther away from the old witch.

"Germani means of the Black Forest. A common enough name in those parts. Now if you'll excuse me. I have duties to carry out for milady."

Elspeth cackled, and the knife and fork left on the plate rattled. "About time. I'll never get that five minutes of my life back, but at least my granddaughter's satisfied." Elspeth slid out and tapped a foot on the floor, waiting for Xandie to move.

Scooting past the witch with a sideways glance, the fae hot-footed it to the dining room exit. He opened the door, then turned back toward Xandie at the last moment. "It is in everyone's best interest that you return the ring. The attempts on your life will stop when milady finally has her property back."

"I'll keep that in mind."

The fae nodded and took a step forward and jerked to a stop as Milly Stabler and Horace Painter opened the door to the bar and stepped into the hallway opposite.

Tyr Greenhand ducked his head and turned sharply to his right, heading up the stairs at a quick clip.

"Xandie." The lavender-haired older woman adjusted her black-rimmed glasses and lunged forward, grabbing the Librarian's hands. "I am so sorry Sabine banned you and your family. You didn't deserve that. I'm sure you had nothing to do with the hex bag in the catering tent or anyone getting sick."

"Milly tried to talk Sabine out of it. But that clipboard woman is ice-cold," Horace added.

Patting Xandie's hand, Milly tried to comfort the Librarian. "This will work out. You just have to put all the puzzle pieces together. After seeing you at the fair over the last week, I have confidence you will do the right thing." Milly dropped Xandie's hand and linked arms with Horace. "We must be going. This is the fair's last day, and there's still plenty to do." Milly's green eyes glittered behind her black-rimmed glasses.

"Thanks."

"By the way, dear. There's a certain foreign bear shifter currently drinking his weight in alcohol at the Mayweather bar. If one wanted information, this would be a perfect time to gather it." Milly winked.

Xandie waved the older couple off and spun to Elspeth. "You wait here. For some reason, people are scared to talk to me when you're around. I'll speak to Eric myself."

"Your funeral, Library Girl." Elspeth buffed her nails on her bony chest. "And I'll have you know I'm a hit at parties. Just look at your karaoke engagement."

Xandie rolled her eyes and pushed open the bar door. Sure enough, Eric Braun propped the bar up with an impressive assortment of empty glasses in front of him. As the door shut behind her, a muted murmur followed by a high-pitched shriek sounded, then was cut off by the closing door.

Whatever carnage Elspeth had just caused, she'd handle it later. She had one inebriated German bear shifter to deal with.

Time for some answers.

EIGHTEEN

"Fancy meeting you here." Xandie slid on to a barstool next to Eric Braun. She poked at one of the empty glasses lined up in front of him. "Drowning your sorrows?"

Eric let out a large belch and slumped in his chair. "Some things require alcoholic sustenance to work through."

Xandie nodded. "Grief takes many forms. As long as the alcohol doesn't become a crutch and you don't hurt anyone drinking yourself insensible."

"Grief." Eric snorted, then drained another glass. He flicked a finger at the bartender, who swiftly placed another full glass in front of him.

"You aren't grieving for Sofie?" Okay, she'd been abrasive and not the nicest bear in Point Muse, but she was still his sister.

"Hard to grieve for one you only met a few times." Eric took a long swallow.

"I'm missing something, aren't I?" She had a nasty feeling Elspeth wouldn't react well to whatever Eric was about to tell Xandie.

He raised his glass in a salute and winked at Xandie. "There's plenty you're missing, little Librarian. The biggest being stealing that ring back and selling it to its original owner. You *have* heard it doesn't belong to the Brauns?"

"People keep telling me that." Xandie rolled her eyes. "Restore honor. Blah, blah, blah."

Eric nodded. "That would be the case with the German Brauns, and there definitely is a lot of blah, blah."

"You talk like you're not part of the family."

"I'm a bear shifter, and I do have some Braun blood but not a direct line like that old woman would like you to think."

There it is. Mathilde had put one over on the Point Muse Brauns and the Harrows. Elspeth would pitch a fit when she found out. "Let me guess. Sofie isn't your sister, and Mathilde isn't your grandmother."

"A distant cousin. Mathilde thought it would be better to show a solid powerbase and that a strong male would achieve that."

"Sofie and Mathilde are related though?"

He nodded. "Mathilde is her grandmother. They are the only ones of the Black Forest Brauns who care about the ring. The rest of the family have moved on and focused on the cuckoo clock business. Mathilde and Sofie think they are better and restoring the ring will make it so."

Xandie wasn't surprised. The late Sofie had always thought she was better than everyone else, and Mathilde was just plain mean. "Why do it? What did you get out of it?"

Eric looked shame faced. "Free trip to America and a bonus if the ring is returned to the fae owner. No bonus if somebody else returns it first."

A solid thump on the wooden bar door distracted

Xandie for a moment. She turned back to Eric. "Sofie wasn't out to restore Braun honor. Not really. She wanted to keep everything for herself."

Eric sighed and pushed his almost empty glass away. "I caught her meeting that jewelry maker from the fair. She brushed it off as casual, but I knew there was more to it. She'd sneak out from the inn at night to meet him. I followed her once and tried to listen in. It was all mumbo-jumbo about rightful inheritance, taking the place at the forefront, not hiding in the shadows any longer. That kind of garbage. Sofie lapped it up. I should have told Mathilde, but Sofie made me promise not to." He stared wistfully off into the distance. "I would have liked to have a sister."

Poor guy. Caught in the middle of two manipulative bear shifters. "Did you ever see Simon hurt Sofie?"

"No." Eric jerked up straight on his stool. "If I'd seen that, I would have stopped it immediately."

Xandie patted the bear on his broad shoulders. "There was nothing you could have done, Eric. This isn't your fault."

Another thump sounded at the bar door followed by an inhumanely high shriek. Xandie sighed and clambered off the barstool. Whatever had happened outside had obviously progressed to carnage if the shrieks are anything to go by. Time for an Elspeth intervention. "Eric, if you need anything, Harrow House will be open to you. And the Point Muse Brauns will understand if you tell the truth. You're still family, after all."

Eric nodded and pushed his glass away. "Thank you, Librarian." He stood and swayed before correcting himself. "I think it's a good time to rest in my room now."

"I wish I could rest in my room," Xandie muttered as she stood in front of the visibly shaking wooden door.

Taking a deep breath, she slammed the door open and was greeted by an explosion of pink mayhem.

Xandie covered her eyes for a moment before cracking one open. She shuddered at the bright pink image assaulting her senses. A large, cotton-candy pink cloud pressed Mathilde Braun against the inn's wood-paneled wall. The elderly shifter's gray, no-nonsense, short bob stood straight up like she'd stuck her fingers into an electricity outlet. With her wooden walking-stick in one hand, Mathilde flailed at the pink cloud crushing her. Skinny legs in pale gray tights and large orthopedic shoes stuck out from the bottom of the cloud.

"How do you like them pink apples?" Elspeth crowed from her perch on top of the reception desk.

Pink foam covered the floor up to the first step of the staircase and oozed over Xandie's shoes and ankles. She quickly turned and slammed the bar door closed in Eric's shocked face. "Sorry," she yelled through the door. "I don't want the Elspeth mayhem to spread."

Taking a deep breath, Xandie turned to her grandmother. "Any words of explanation? This time?"

"Never pick a fight with someone meaner than you?" Elspeth cackled and clapped her hands. A portion of the pink cotton candy foam bubbled like a wicked witch's potion in front of Elspeth.

Rubbing her forehead, Xandie sighed. "In other words, Mathilde said something you didn't like, and you pink cloud slimed her."

"Exactly." Elspeth winked. "Apparently, it's all your fault her poor Sofie died. If you hadn't stolen the ring, this would never have happened."

Red heat flushed up Xandie's throat. She'd never stolen anything in her life. *How dare that old bear...* "For your information, this whole situation is Goldi Locks' fault. She stole the ring, not me. And if you hadn't been so focused on getting one over on the American Brauns and pocketing a nice finder's fee, everything would have been fine. And FYI, your sainted Sofie was meeting the enemy and had planned to double-cross you." Xandie wound down, breathless. *Oops.* Maybe she shouldn't have said that, but Harrows weren't exactly known for their placid natures.

Mathilde stopped flailing at the cloud and growled. Her fingers turned to claws. She dropped her walking stick to the ground in her shifter rage. "How dare you. Sofie was my granddaughter. She would never cross me. Unlike you disloyal Harrows."

Oh no, she didn't... "Let's talk about disloyalty. How about the fact Eric isn't Sofie's brother or even your grandson?" Xandie stalked forward through the pink foam. "You're so obsessed with getting a reward, you can't see what's in front of you."

"Say what?" Elspeth shrieked and joined Xandie in glaring at the pink-cloud-bound Mathilde. "You snuck in a ringer? You're pitiful."

"Pitiful?" Mathilde roared as a monobrow sprouted across her forehead. Her skin rippled as she forced a change.

"Bring it, you hairy bear loser." Elspeth rubbed her hands together and flexed her muscles. "I put you in a pink bubble jail once. I can do it again."

"My inn!" Rose Mayweather stood on the staircase and shrieked as she stared at the pink-painted reception area. "What have you all done?"

"That's what I'd like to know." Zach Braun stood in the inn's entrance, his mother close behind. Both bears gazed in shock at the pink sea covering the floor.

"Leg it. It's the fuzz. Every Harrow witch for herself." Elspeth jumped down from her perch and tried to run for the bar door but instead slipped, landing face down in pink foam. The only part of her body showing was a tangled clump of raven-black wig. She rolled over and spat out a mouthful of pink foam. "Well, if I'm stuck, I might as well enjoy myself." She opened and closed her legs, pretending she was a snow angel in pink foam.

"Look what you've done to my poor inn." Rose stamped her foot. "Throw the book at her, Chief Braun."

"Elspeth, stop swimming in the foam and release Mrs. Braun immediately." Zach growled the order.

"She threw the first claw, not me. I just contained her. You should be thanking me." Elspeth sat up, pink bubbles coating her clothing.

"I don't care how it started, I'm ending it." Zach turned to Xandie. "Anything to add, Ms. Meyers?"

Formality is a bad sign. "Only that the bear had it coming. Sneaking a stranger in, claiming he's her grandson, and carrying out a plan to steal my engagement ring and sell it back to its original owner? I'd say we're the injured party here."

Agatha Braun, a.k.a. Elspeth's crony, a.k.a. Zach's mother, shot past her son and windmilled her arms as she slid in the pink foam. Catching her balance, she frowned. "What do you mean, harboring a charlatan?"

"He's not a charlatan. He *is* a German Braun. True blood and hearty stock, unlike you weak Americans." Mathilde sneered, her monobrow settling back into two separate furry caterpillars.

"But he isn't your grandson. He might be of Braun blood, but he's not a direct bloodline." Elspeth's top lip curled. "So, liar, liar, pants on fire."

"That's enough. Let her down, Elspeth, and clean up this mess."

"And if I don't, copper? What are you gonna do?" Elspeth roared back.

The police chief stepped inside and let his three deputies file in, spelled handcuffs at the ready. "Then we're taking a ride to the station to sort this out."

Elspeth held out her wrists, amber eyes flashing maliciously as one of Zach's younger brothers carefully pulled the wicked witch to her feet. "Sleep with one eye open, Zachary Braun. One eye."

All fight drained from Xandie as Melody, Zach's younger sister, snapped on a set of her very own spelled handcuffs.

Lunch turned out awesome. What will dinner be like?

NINETEEN

"I'm on a hunger strike." Elspeth crossed her arms and glared at the chicken pot pie.

Xandie used her knife to lift the pastry lid off her pie, gagging at the beige mix of meat underneath.

"Too proud to eat the food given to you?" Mathilde shook her head and shoved in a mouthful, chewing determinedly. The bear shifter's face soured like she'd bitten into a lemon. She spat the mouthful into her napkin and put it back on her tray.

"Too proud?" Elspeth retorted mockingly.

"What is that?" Mathilde pointed a finger at the chicken pot pie.

"It was Caleb's turn to cook. He chose to nuke the pies in the microwave for you," Melody offered with a wince. "At least the meals are in date. I did check that." Riley was still at the inn to help clean up the pink mess.

"I think Aggie needs to give him cooking lessons. This is a crime against humanity." Xandie shuddered and pushed the meal away. "I think I'll join the hunger strike."

"Probably safer," Melody agreed. She stepped closer to

the bars. "Zach figures if he puts you all in the same holding cell, you'd work out your issues without him getting involved."

"Does he just?" Elspeth strolled to the bars and ran her metal cup over them, creating a musical racket. "Hear that? I will not give in. I will nurse my grievance. No making up."

Mathilde pushed herself to her feet and lumbered over to the bars on the other side of the cell. "I hesitate to agree with the obnoxious witch, but my enmity will never die. My grudge will go to the grave." She added her cup to the musical protests.

"Ha." Elspeth did a jerky dance on the spot. "Even the old bear knows I'm right."

"Settle down, Harrows and Braun." Zach strolled into the holding area. "Calmed down, yet?"

Elspeth grabbed her chicken pot pie and shoved it at the bars. "This is cruel and unusual punishment. How dare you try to poison me, Zachary Braun?"

Zach grimaced. "Mom really needs to teach Caleb to cook."

Melody shuddered. Her muscular shoulders twitched, and she scratched the back of her neck with a brightly painted pink nail. "Could you suggest that when I'm not around? The mess he creates in the kitchen makes me cry."

"It makes everyone cry." Zach drew a set of keys out of his pocket and unlocked the cell door. "Time to leave, ladies. The other occupants of the cells have demanded your release. Apparently, they can't stand the squabbling any longer." He opened the door wide. "Please leave my cells and never come back. Unless you're disorderly, and then you're straight back here and eating Caleb's cooking, got it?" He focused on Elspeth. "Does everyone hear me?"

Elspeth rolled her eyes. "Geez. The whole cell block can hear you."

"Yeah, and we agree with the cops," a voice yelled from farther down.

Mathilde grunted and pushed her way past Zach and Melody. "I hope never to see Point Muse again. This whole town is cursed."

Stepping aside, Elspeth waved the shifter through first. "Wizened age before beauty."

Melody snickered and then hid her laughter with a fake coughing fit. "Why don't I see you out, Mrs. Braun." Melody quickly took the bear shifter's arm and guided her out, leaving Xandie and Elspeth in the cell block.

Zach pointedly turned his back on the wicked witch of Point Muse to focus on Xandie. "I heard a rumor you might have illegally obtained a certain ledger."

Xandie swallowed the lump in her throat. *Curse the effectiveness of Point Muse gossip.* "I can neither confirm nor deny that."

Leaning closer, Zach's breath feathered Xandie's cheek. "If said ledger was to turn up at your Library and some civic-minded Librarian were to secure it safely, Point Muse law enforcement would be grateful. If that Librarian was then to remain home tonight instead of wandering around town breaking and entering, law enforcement could take possession of the currently missing ledger." Zach stole a quick kiss. "I'd be happy, too."

"Anything to make my fiancé happy, including the fact I hypothetically may have lined up a translator for the ledger." Xandie returned his kiss.

"Aww, man. Will you two can it? It's worse than listening to that old witch belly ache about dinner," the same voice from before yelled out.

Elspeth popped her head back into the cell area. "Did someone just call me old?" She pointed to Braun and Xandie. "Skedaddle, kiddies, I got a mouthy jailbird to deal with." She pushed the other two out of the cell area and slammed the door behind them. A howl sounded just after a popping noise.

"Not the stink bomb. Not. The. Stink. Bomb," someone wailed from behind the closed door.

Xandie sidled toward the exit. "You know what? I think it's time to leave."

Braun spun toward his fiancée. "Don't you dare. Only rats desert a sinking ship."

"Only rats and Harrows." Making a squeaking noise like a rat, Xandie scuttled out of the station without a backward glance. She'd rather deal with a killer on the prowl than a rabid, hex-mad Elspeth. It was all about priorities.

"Kid, you're getting quite a rap sheet. I'm impressed." Colin gnawed on a bone Holly had obligingly placed on the floor of the Library. "Of course, my dame probably had something to do with it."

Xandie slumped into a large, comfortable chair close to the fire the Library had left for her. It wasn't winter yet, but the nights were getting cooler.

"Elspeth and Mathilde caused it. I was an innocent bystander." She pointed at Charlie. "Why didn't the super spy get us out?"

Charlie snickered. "A few hours in the local lock-up is character building. Besides, covert, remember?"

"It's always Elspeth's fault anyway. Best not to get other people involved in the mayhem." Lila swallowed the last mouthful of her lobster spaghetti. "And once I heard it was Caleb's turn to cook at the station, I decided to deliver the spaghetti." She shuddered. "No one deserves his cooking."

"Thanks, Lila. My stomach appreciates it. Elspeth's back at Harrow House, so at least she doesn't get rewarded for bad behavior."

"That we know of," Holly pointed out. "She's sneaky. We don't currently know what she's up to."

Lila placed the empty plate on a desk. "That's why I'm the smartest Harrow. I made Nash keep an eye out for her. You can't trust Colin because she always bribes him with food." She pointed an accusing finger at the pug. "I figured with Colin out of Harrow House, she wouldn't have a minion to cover her tracks."

Charlie licked her fork, then pushed her plate away. "Using the hound was a good plan."

"Hate to break this to you, girls, but Nash has a thing about icing. My girl has a stash of colored icing for whenever she needs Nash to look the other way." Colin burped. "Haven't you wondered about all that weight he's been gaining lately?"

"What?" Lila screeched and collapsed against the couch, thumping herself on the chest dramatically. "That traitor. He stabs me through the heart. Time for an icing-free diet. He will suffer for his sins."

"It's Elspeth. She's evil. Knows all our weaknesses. You can't really blame him. It's Elspeth, she manipulates everyone." Holly nodded to back up her words.

"Aren't you little Miss Sunshine?" Xandie threw a cushion at the banshee. "Death's stalking us. Why haven't you wailed, banshee?"

Holly glared at Xandie and dumped the cushion on the floor. "I don't always wail at every death or possible death.

You know my gift is erratic and it's linked to the Harrows. At least we think it is. Maybe nobody wants to kill you guys yet?"

"Kill us?" Lila objected. "What about you?"

"I don't go around upsetting people or sliming them with pink foam."

"Girl's got a point," Colin added helpfully. He pushed his bone away and rolled onto his back. "Getting off the subject of killing Harrows, who wants to give me some pats? I'm feeling unloved since my goddess of mayhem isn't here."

Charlie poked the pug with a toe. "No offense, but maybe it's time Elspeth placed the pug on his own diet."

Colin rolled over and batted at the perky super-spook's toe. "Don't swear at me. I've banned the word from Harrow House. Such expletives should not cross a well-bred dame's lips."

"Hate to agree with Elspeth's minion, but I kinda side with him." Xandie loved her hot chocolate, but if she wanted to fit into her wedding dress, a judicious application of willpower regarding sweets might have to be applied. And she hated the idea. She was with Colin. Diet was a swear word.

"When is Chief Fiancé rocking up to get Simon's ledger?" Holly stood and drifted around the Library, peering out the window and trailing fingers along the shelves.

"Any minute now. Are you checking my housekeeping skills?"

Shaking her head, Holly leaned against the Library's large bay window that looked out onto the back garden and the bluff. "I don't know, I just feel unsettled. Like something or someone is coming. Bad vibes, I guess."

Xandie moved to stand next to her cousin at the

window. The security lights at the back illuminated a small pool of light over the central garden and the statues of the nine Muses who'd helped form the Library. "It's Point Muse, so bad vibes are an everyday thing." She squinted at a dark cloud racing toward them. "Are we supposed to get storms tonight?"

Lila joined her cousins at the window. "No. All clear tonight. Unless Elspeth's playing with the weather now?"

"That's a no-no. Elspeth always says only fools play with mother nature and she ain't no fool."

"Except when she made you?"

Colin nodded at Lila. "Exactly. Whatever's heading our way isn't Elspeth-caused. You might want to batten the hatches and gird your loins."

"Hearing gird your loins from a pug's mouth just feels wrong," Lila muttered but carefully stepped a pace away from the window.

"The Library's got this. Its security protocols won't let anything in... *I hope.* Besides, it's probably just a freak storm."

Holly rested a hand on the window, frowning. "I have a feeling." She turned and stared at her cousins. Silver flickered through her normally amber eyes. *"Something's coming."*

"That's creepy, even for Point Muse." Charlie shivered.

"Stand down, banshee." Lila slapped a hand on a desk, the noise ricocheting around the Library.

Silver seeped away and Holly's eyes returned to their normal amber. A bang sounded from the window. Holly snatched a hand away as more loud bangs sounded from the glass.

The door to the Library slammed open, and Theo, Xandie's black cat guardian, came galloping in, skidding to a stop next to a now cowering Colin. "Activate security, the Library's under attack. Who did you upset now?"

"Why is it always our fault? Anyone think to blame the homicidal maniac attacking us?" Xandie crept closer to the window, peering out. "What *is* attacking us?"

Holly screeched and pointed to the outside windowsill. "*Bugs.* I did not sign up for bugs." She dropped behind the couch, only her eyes and the top of her head showing.

"Such bravery." Charlie smirked and rolled up her sleeves.

Lila slowly moved back in line with Holly. "I'm kind of with the banshee on this."

The tempo of bugs hitting the window with a staccato of metallic clangs increased. A screeching noise sounded at the base of the window as several silver cockroaches crawled along the glass, scratching at the window with their legs, leaving thin slices behind. The bugs scattered all over the window and a large pile of metallic bodies grew underneath the windowsill.

"This might be a good time to swing into action, Library." The Library always protected the Librarian, even from metal bugs. Hopefully. The building shuddered, and the massive bugs that fell away from the window were soon replaced. Blue electricity flickered over the building, wreathing it in a colorful blue protection, but the sheer mass of bugs began to overwhelm the light show.

Theo let out a yowl and scooted behind the couch with Holly.

Colin joined the cowardly duo and Lila scooted in next to him.

"Maybe the metal is too much for the Library to handle? Could we beef up the magic somehow?" Charlie rushed to a shelf and hauled out a large tome. She hefted the book up in both hands and gave it an experimental swing. "But just in case, this should be strong enough to flatten any metal bugs that make it inside. Weapon up, Harrows, it's time to fight." Charlie chortled and lined up close to the window, ready to swing and destroy.

A tiny crack appeared in the corner of the bay window, slowly creeping diagonally up. "Library?" Xandie's ring tightened and released around her finger. She held up her hand and rubbed the tarnished metal. "If you can help the Library out, I'd really appreciate it." The ring pulsed once, then a second time. A rushing noise just outside the window filled the Library. A forest of green surged across the glass. The metallic thumps dwindled away to nothing as a living wall of grass and flowers covered the window. The interior of the Library suddenly blazed with bright light, as if the Library was relieved at its rescue.

"Thanks, ring," Xandie whispered to the tarnished jewelry.

Charlie carefully placed the book on a side table. "That was anticlimactic. I feel let down." She pouted, bottom lip quivering.

Holly peeped out from behind the couch. "Did the Library save us?"

Theo shook himself and prowled out from his cowardly huddle with the others. "See? I told you not to worry. The Library can deal with anything."

"Actually, it wasn't the Library that saved us. It was the ring." Lila stood and dusted off her jeans. "I see why everyone wants that ugly thing now."

"You think my ring's ugly?" Zach strode into the Library, Deputy Melody at his side.

"Ignore her. She's just jealous she doesn't have a magic

ring." Xandie threw herself at Zach and sighed in relief as his muscled arms closed around her.

"The green wall belongs to the ring?"

Xandie nodded against Zach's muscled chest. "Yep. Apparently, it doesn't like metal bugs attacking us any more than the Library does."

But the fact the attacks were increasing meant Xandie was closing in on the killer...

Watch out, Simon Wald. Sherlock Librarian is on the prowl.

TWENTY

"If I ever see a metal bug again, it's too soon." Holly yawned and huddled over a steaming coffee. "I kept imagining metal cockroaches eating my toes while I slept. Kept me up all night."

"Where I, on the other hand, slept the sleep of the innocent." Lila beamed and settled a hot chocolate in front of Xandie. "What about you, revered Librarian?"

Reaching for her hot chocolate, Xandie savored the scent of rich, sweet, sugary goodness. "Took me a while to get to sleep, but that wasn't because of bad dreams. Theo was practicing for some karaoke competition he and Elspeth are entering. Those high notes are murder." Xandie took a bracing mouthful of hot chocolate, moaning as the rich taste hit the back of her throat.

"Steady there, Librarian." Charlie smirked and sipped her black tea. "I had no issues sleeping. Bugs wouldn't dare nibble my toes." She winked at the cousins. "It would make my bosses sleep better if old Simon snooty killer pants were taken off the mean streets of Point Muse, however."

"I'm working on it." Xandie grimaced. "He's proving suspiciously good at hiding. Maybe that's the fae in him."

"I feel a little bit sorry for him. Imagine if your family had been shunned for decades. Then his parents died, and he was raised by the person who caused the shunning. There must be a bucket-load of negative emotion." Holly sighed. "Makes you appreciate your own family."

"Even Elspeth?" Xandie poked fun at her banshee cousin, but honestly, she could understand what Holly meant. After her own mother had gone missing for so long, Xandie could understand bitterness and recrimination.

"Plenty of people lose their parents and don't end up a homicidal arms dealer and a killer," Charlie pointed out.

"Still sad." Holly stubbornly stuck to her point.

"Whatever, Pollyanna." Charlie jiggled in her seat. "What's our next step? Is it time for action yet?"

Xandie rolled her eyes. "Your last name should be Harrow, not Locks. You're a clone of Elspeth."

"Thank you." Charlie beamed at Xandie but sobered a little. "We still need to work out where we go from here. None of us can afford for Simon Wald or Schwartzwald, whatever his name is, to get away."

"I'm working on it."

Milly and Horace wandered into Lila's bakery, smiling faces turned to each other. Milly drew up in front of Xandie's table. "Xandie dear. How are you?" She placed a comforting hand on the younger woman's shoulder. "I heard about the attack last night. So scary."

Point Muse gossip strikes again. "How did you hear so quickly?"

"Oh, sweetie. It's Point Muse. I heard about it as soon as I stepped into town with Horace this morning."

"We're fine. Turns out we have a secret weapon." Xandie glanced at the ring.

"Ah, yes. The fabled engagement ring. Another topic the gossips are in a lather over. May I have a look at it?"

Taking the ring off, Xandie held it up to the older woman.

Recoiling, Milly shook her head. "No. No. I don't want to touch it. Bad luck and all that. If you could just hold your hand up. An engagement ring should always stay with the one it's intended for."

Horace wiped his forehead, sweat standing out on the pale skin as he stared worriedly at Milly.

"Okay." Strange reaction for the old man to have. Almost as if he was worried for his lavender-haired girlfriend. Xandie slipped the ring back onto her finger and lifted a hand into the air, showing off the ring.

Milly leaned in close and considered the tarnished jewelry. "It's certainly striking with those unappealing black spots, but some silver is poking through. I really do like the etched roses that are beginning to show. It doesn't look out of place on your hand." Milly smiled. "You fit the ring, or the ring fits you, it seems."

Xandie lowered her hand to the tabletop. "Apparently it belongs to someone else. Seems like everyone wants it."

Milly pursed her lips. "It may officially belong to another, and I'll admit it does have the look of fae jewelry, but in the end, it's on your finger. You get to decide what happens to it."

Snorting, Xandie took a quick sip of her hot chocolate. "A couple of dead bodies and a rampaging killer suggests not."

Milly trilled a laugh. "That will sort itself out. Just stay true to yourself." She leveled a serious gaze at Xandie. "Be careful. If it is of fae design, they are a law unto themselves. The ring may have gifts but never count on it or expect help. Fae artifacts can be moody and flighty. It's best to be polite when dealing with the ring." Warning done, Milly linked arms with Horace. "Now we need to order. I have a fierce craving for Lila's cupcakes. Ta-ta, dear." She smiled warmly at the table before heading to the bakery counter with Horace in tow.

"Seems word of last night's attack and the ring's magic has already spread beyond Point Muse." Lila collected empty plates. "Matthew called me from Portland this morning. He wanted to make sure we were safe."

"Not surprising he heard. He's a reaper and we've had multiple deaths. Does he know the reaper who had to collect the souls?" Matthew Grim had been appointed the reaper for Point Muse because of the rising levels of supernatural deaths in town. Point Muse... the murder capital of the supernatural world. Not something that drew the tourists in.

"One of his dad's friends, apparently. The reaper world has been elevated to priority level. They expect more death in Point Muse imminently unless Simon's caught. Matthew's on his way back already." Lila smiled down at Nash as he wandered out of the kitchen and collapsed under the table. "Nash is missing him. He'll be glad to get Matthew back."

"Maybe I should warn my bosses about more business." Holly nibbled on a cookie. "They hate it when they get rush jobs. They like to take their time."

Xandie shuddered at the thought of a funeral home rush job. "There's no need. Everything will be fine. We have it handled."

The door to Lila's bakery slammed open. Eric Braun

stood panting, his large bear shifter frame shuddering as if he'd run a mile. "Librarian. We have a problem."

Xandie pushed her hot chocolate away and glowered around the bakery. "It's like the gods hate me. Or maybe they're pranking me." She blew out a gusty breath. "Okay, Eric. What happened?"

"Mathilde's missing from the inn. She was having tea on the porch with a guest. I went to fetch something from her room and found it a mess. Like someone had searched it and turned it over. I returned to the porch to inform her, but she and her guest had disappeared. The table and chairs were on their sides and loose metal parts were scattered around."

An awful feeling of dread crept along Xandie's spine. Her Harrow tingle, as Lila called it, was currently zapping electric shocks along her nerve endings. Xandie had no choice, she had to ask. "The guest Mathilde had for tea. Was it Elspeth?"

Eric swallowed, his face pasty white, before nodding.

Lila pinched the bridge of her nose. "Elspeth probably goaded the metal kidnappers into taking her. She'd have been offended if they'd taken just Mathilde and not her as well."

"I really need a holiday from kidnapping," Holly moaned and shoved another cookie into her mouth, chewing furiously.

Xandie stood and dusted off her hands. "We really need to take out kidnapping insurance." At least it wasn't her turn this time.

"You Harrows need to take out kidnapping insurance." Rose stood on the porch, arms folded, glaring at Xandie and her cousins as they arrived at the inn.

"I just said that." Xandie turned to Holly. "Didn't I just say that?"

Holly grimaced. "Sadly, you did." She brightened. "Mind you, think of all the money we can make out of Elspeth every time some misguided idiot thinks they can take her on. We'd be rich."

"Or maybe we just shut Elspeth in Harrow House and never let her out again," Xandie muttered.

"Why punish me? What have I done to you?" Holly poked her tongue out at her cousin and then crouched next to a broken teacup. She fished around in the ceramic mess and drew out a curved metal claw. "Look familiar?"

"Hecate's bug exterminator," Xandie cursed and clomped up the stairs to stand next to Holly. "What happened?"

Rose sighed. "Elspeth showed up an hour ago, wanting to sit down with that mouthy Braun bear sow. They both demanded tea and sat out on the porch." Rose sniffed. "Elspeth implied I'm an eavesdropper and that's why they wanted to sit out front."

"Sounds like Elspeth." She probably wanted to sip Witchshine from her hip flask without the inn owner busting her.

"Nothing to do with eavesdropping. Just that addiction to her hip flask." Rose shook her head. The silver-streaked blonde's upswept hairdo wobbled precariously.

"They were having tea..." Xandie prodded. "Were they fighting?"

"They looked like gossipy old crows," Rose sneered. "But they weren't fighting, just sipping their Witchshine spiked tea. I couldn't get close enough to hear what they were discussing, so I headed inside. I'm not sure how much time passed, but I heard a crash from outside. I assumed Elspeth and that bear were brawling."

Eric shuffled from foot to foot. "I think they were talking about alliances. And about taking over the Black Forest. Stuff like that. There was a lot of cackling before I went inside."

Xandie rolled her eyes. She wouldn't have put it past Elspeth to pop one on the feisty bear shifter's nose along with an insult or five. But a rumble at morning tea wasn't first on Elspeth's list of mayhem causing antics. *World domination, on the other hand...* "But you didn't see them fighting, Rose?"

"Nope. When I investigated, I found my third-best china smashed, the furniture turned over, and those old women missing. I assumed it was another Harrow issue and rang your fiancé." Rose smirked at Xandie, Lila, and Holly. "One does need to include one's significant other in this kind of sensitive issue, you know." She fluttered her thick, fake eyelashes. "And look, here's our delicious police chief now." Beaming, Rose minced past Xandie, the innkeeper's pink petticoats pushing Xandie to the side.

"What's Elspeth done now?" Zack slammed the door of his police cruiser shut and joined the others on the porch.

"I think she got herself and Mathilde kidnapped." Xandie pointed to the disarray on the porch.

"How on earth did anyone manage to take Elspeth alive?"

Holly picked up an unbroken teacup, sniffed it, and handed it to the police chief. "Looks like they were drugged."

"Nonsense." Rose glared at the banshee. "How dare you

impugn my establishment? No, I run a drug and kidnapping free place here. It's a rule."

"Except for today," Xandie pointed out.

"Today doesn't count. I trust my staff implicitly. They wouldn't drug customers. Not even Elspeth Harrow."

"And her hip flask never leaves Elspeth's sight. It has to be in the food or the tea."

Zack nodded at his fiancée. "And if it wasn't an employee, then a customer must've poisoned them. Everyone was on the lookout for Simon, so it's possible he may have enlisted someone else's help."

A woman called the inn owner back and Rose bustled inside.

Holly grabbed Xandie's hand and held tight. "Elspeth wouldn't have gone without a fight, even being drugged. What if she's hurt?"

Xandie squeezed Holly's hand. "She'll make Simon wish he'd never been born. We'll find them." She released Holly's hand and waggled her fingers. "Besides, we all know what he's after."

Rose rushed back out and shoved a piece of paper in Xandie's face. "One of my employees just took this over the phone. This is the extent of my help. I'm done. I want nothing to do with hostages."

Xandie snatched the paper from Rose, who hustled back inside the inn, slamming the door shut behind her. "Tell us how you really feel." She opened the message and read it aloud. "You know who I have and what I want. The fair, ten p.m. tonight, big tent."

Zack cursed. "That's confirmation. I need to notify the Paranormal Investigative Group that we have a supernatural hostage situation."

Charlie stepped out from the side of the inn. "Sorry for

eavesdropping." She stopped for a moment, head cocked to one side, and smirked. "Actually, I'm not that sorry. My bosses are already aware of the situation and authorize you to work with me." She wiggled her fingers at the open-mouthed police chief.

"What?"

Giggling, Charlie tried to present a sober face. "Charlie Locks, special branch, the Paranormal Investigative Group. Nice to meet ya."

Zach turned slowly to face his fiancée. "You knew she was a PIG? The relative of that killer, Goldi Locks, part of one of the craftiest thieving syndicates in the supernatural world, is an agent?"

"Oops." Xandie shrugged. "Figured she was a spook like mom, but no initials were ever mentioned." She rubbed her fiancé's arm. "Now, be a big bear. You need to learn to play nice with other law enforcement types. The focus is getting Elspeth and Mathilde back. And we all know what we need to do to achieve that." Xandie held up her hand. The little spots of silver on the ring gleamed in the morning light. The black, tarnished patches on the silver were almost completely gone now.

Zach stroked a lock of Xandie's frizzy, brown hair out of her face. "I regret not buying you a simple ring with no baggage attached."

Xandie laid her head on his shoulder. "It's Point Muse and Harrow bad luck. It trumps all good intentions." She stood on tip toes and brushed a kiss over her fiancé's whiskered cheek. "Right now, we need to circle the Harrow wagons and work out how we're going to take down a killer."

Elephants with combat boots line-danced in the pit of Xandie's stomach. Elspeth's life was at risk, and she didn't have time to procrastinate. Simon, the snooty arms dealer, had no clue the can of worms he'd opened. Mess with one Harrow, you mess with them all.

And no one took on Elspeth Harrow and lived to tell the tale...

TWENTY-ONE

"Does anyone else feel like vomiting?" Holly whispered to her cousins as she gripped her hex bag tighter.

"Pretty much. But then I felt like that when we raided the last of Elspeth's hex stock," Xandie whispered. Elspeth was notoriously private and tight-lipped about what her creation cave, a.k.a. her Witchshine shed, contained. Knowing someone, even family, had been in there poking through her stock would send the old witch ballistic. Elspeth on the warpath was never pretty. It was almost as bad as a bored Elspeth.

"Suck it up, buttercup. It's her fault she got nabbed in the first place." Colin shook his puggish head. "I'm so disappointed in her. She really should've taken me to the meeting."

Xandie bit back an inappropriate laugh. Rescue missions shouldn't have excess hilarity. At least not when they involved Elspeth Harrow.

"Mother's used to it." Miranda nudged her daughter's shoulder. "It's okay not to be serious all the time. It's about maintaining adrenaline levels without losing your edge. It's a good plan, now it's time to execute. I'm moving into position." Miranda shouldered her sniper rifle and blended back into the shadows, disappearing completely.

"That woman freaks me out sometimes." Lila cracked her neck. "Are we ready to go yet? I'm getting old just sitting here."

Nash, Lila's hellhound, blew sulfur-scented breath at her. "Pet safe."

Lila growled low in her throat, imitating her hound. "How many times do I have to tell you? I'm not the pet, you are." She poked the hound's nose. "Got it, mutt?"

"Yeah. The kid's got it." Colin paced around Eric, the bear shifter's, feet. "You okay there, bear-boy?"

Eric swallowed and licked his lips. "I've never had to participate in a rescue mission, especially for a maniacal distant relative. I find it vaguely upsetting."

Xandie shrugged. "You get used to it. We have a plan. You're the muscle for Colin, and Nash is there if you need backup. No sudden moves and hide yourself until the signal. We don't want any premature detonations."

Xandie fixed the pug with a no-nonsense stare. "Remember, not until go time. Got it, Colin?"

"Yeah, worrywart. *Colin-the-man* has everything under control. Seafood has been consumed, the weapon is primed and ready. Come on, boys. Tally-ho. Time to rescue my damsel in distress." Colin trotted off to his position, Nash and Eric in tow.

Thank Hecate Theo had refused to come. He had a karaoke competition coming up and refused to risk his throat in the cold air. Any more smart-mouthed animals would drive Xandie crazy.

"You know we're all going to regret Colin eating seafood, don't you?"

Xandie glared at Holly. "You wanted a plan. So, we planned everything out... *Ad nauseam*. Don't diss the plan now that we're ready to roll."

Holly backed away, hands up. "Geez. On edge much? I'm just saying, we're Harrows. Nothing ever goes to plan. Be prepared for chaos and mayhem. Especially if the wicked witch of Point Muse is involved."

"I planned for every contingency. The fair's shut down and deserted. Zach and his deputies are hiding, ready to take Simon into custody and provide back-up. Mom is on perimeter and sniper duty. Charlie's already inside, hidden. The animals and Eric are primed if we need the ultimate takedown, and you guys have your hex bombs. We're good to go."

A small cough had Xandie turning hurriedly. Milly and Horace, plus the fae, Tyr Greenhand, stood behind them. "And Milly, Horace, and Mr. Greenhand, I hear you're helping with camouflage. Sorry, I forgot you," Xandie apologized to the trio.

Milly waved away the words. "Nonsense. We're happy to be involved."

"It's been a long time since I've been on a mission. I'd forgotten what it felt like." Horace beamed. "I was search and rescue in my younger days when I had a full head of hair."

Tyr Greenhand ran a finger around the collar of his black knit shirt. "Yes. We are quite ready." He shot a sneaking glance at Milly, who ignored him. "I'm aware of my obligations and will endeavor to make sure the foliage in the area will cover the tent, both inside and outside, making escape difficult and containing the threat. Milly and Horace will guard my back."

He parroted the words Xandie had used earlier to

explain the plan. Milly and Horace had offered to keep an eye on the fae. They had orders to pull him out if the rescue didn't go to plan.

"Don't worry, dear." Milly winked at Xandie. "Your plan is solid. Lots of parts, but everyone knows what to do. We'll protect Mr. Greenhand."

"Quite." Tyr appeared momentarily scandalized at the idea.

"I'm sure this will go to plan." Horace patted the fae on his back with two large thumps. "Come on, fae boy. Let's get you into position." Horace nodded to Xandie and grabbed Tyr's arm, towing him into the dark.

Milly lingered for a moment. "Just trust your instincts. There's a reason the Library picked you."

"My love of books, chocolate, and snark?" Inappropriate humor was the hallmark of the Harrows and kept Xandie's nerves steady.

"Exactly." Milly blew Xandie a kiss and blended into the shadows.

"There are way too many people here. Normally it's just us charging to the rescue," Lila complained. "At least Grim, Aunt Winnie, and Mom are back at Harrow House in case Simon bolts and targets it. Any more people out here and we could have a party."

"Stop whining, Lila." Holly nudged her cousin. "Xandie's playing it safe. She's doing the right thing for once. Never doubt a good plan."

The grass around the tent quivered and surged higher. That was the signal. "Right. It's started. You guys get into place. It's go time." Xandie waited for her cousins to disappear before letting out a deep breath. "Everything will be fine. You planned for every contingency. Snap out of it, Xandie." So why did it feel all wrong? Simon wanted the ring in exchange for the hostages. Xandie was supposed to lure him out and then *bam*...her crew would take down the villain and rescue the hostages. "But it doesn't feel right." She had a horrible premonition her plan was doomed to fail. *What did Milly say?* Use your instincts. The Library picked you for a reason. Making a snap decision, Xandie lifted the ring up to her mouth and whispered, "If you help me tonight, I swear I'll give you back to your rightful owner. What do you say?" The ring stayed stubbornly quiet. "Please? This is my family. Do a Librarian a solid. The Library and I will owe you a favor. How about that?"

The ring pulsed twice on Xandie's finger and then quieted.

"Everyone has an ulterior motive." She dropped her hand and took a succession of calming breaths. Everyone watching the tent was about to lose their collective mind. "The best thing about a good plan is knowing when to ignore it." Xandie prowled toward the tent. She paused at the tent flap as a prickly, thorny vine slid inside ahead of her, and a green carpet shot up outside. Tyr had handled his part of the plan.

Xandie stepped in, letting the flap fall closed behind her. A puddle of light illuminated the chair-bound Elspeth and Mathilde, with a maniacally grinning Simon standing behind them, holding a long, slender, glistening hatpin at Elspeth's neck.

"Well, well. I'm quite surprised you decided to confront me. I assumed you'd lure me outside and your posse of law enforcement would take me down somehow. Of course, I have planned for the situation."

Simon, the snooty arms dealer, knew the plan. Thankfully, Xandie was a Harrow and the plan had gone out the window. She risked a quick glance around the tent. Vines wriggled around the edge of the room, currently covered by shadows. Out of the corner of her eye, Xandie spotted the green carpet from outside shooting up the tent's interior walls until it resembled a green cave.

"Cat got your tongue, Librarian? I'm quite disappointed. I expected more from the Harrows and the vaunted Librarian to the supernatural Great Library of Alexandria."

"Sucks when reality slaps you in the face, doesn't it, Mr. Schwartzwald?"

"Touché, Ms. Meyers. You finally found out who I am. Should I be impressed?"

As Xandie stepped closer, she spotted a shadow that quivered. *Charlie,* already in position. She chose to go with the flow and hoped it wouldn't get her or the hostages killed. "It must've been horrible. Your grandfather's people shunning your family. Then you lost your parents and had to move. Of course, your grandfather would have been bitter. And now he's forced you to commit murder. It's sad."

"Sad?" Simon spat out the word. "What's sad is watching my family suffer. This will restore our glory, our honor."

"Say it, don't spray it." Elspeth grimaced. "Villain-monologuing is boring."

Mathilde glared at the elderly witch. "What's boring is being stuck here. If I'd known a little harmless plotting would result in us being bound to chairs next to each other, I'd have avoided the meeting. *I blame you, Elspeth Harrow,*" Mathilde bellowed Elspeth's last name.

"You wanted help to annex the Black Forest. I just offered you an alliance. You wanted to meet with me. It's your own greed that got you here, bear," Elspeth roared back.

"Shut it, old women," Simon screeched. His hatpin wobbled precariously close to Elspeth's neck. "I'm sick of you. All you do is pick at each other."

Elspeth winked at Xandie. Shadows thickened around the tent, blending with the creeping nature and covering Charlie completely.

"Welcome to my world of Elspeth-caused chaos." Xandie shook her head. Elspeth could try the patience of a saint.

"Enough," Simon bellowed. "Did you think I wouldn't notice nature creeping into the tent? That ridiculous fae Greenhand's work, I take it?" He inched the hatpin closer to Elspeth's throat. "Did I mention this is poisoned with Wolfsbane? Call off your dogs now, and give me the ring, or I swear I'll kill her."

The vial Elspeth had pocketed must have had Wolfsbane in it. Xandie pretended to think about it before shaking her head. "You know what? I don't think so." She lifted the hand that she'd concealed next to her leg and let loose one of Elspeth's smoke hex bombs. The balloon burst at her grandmother's feet and wreathed Simon and the hostages immediately in smoke, obscuring their bodies.

A grunt sounded twice, one after the other. On each side, a still-bound hostage had fallen to the ground and pulled themselves bit by excruciating bit out of the smoke cloud, their wooden chairs still attached.

Elspeth muttered a low curse and dragged herself back into the vision-obscuring cloud.

"Now," Xandie bellowed.

Lila and Holly came from opposite sides of the tent and threw their balloons. Pink and green smoke exploded, covering the immediate area in a smoky kaleidoscope of color.

A loud roar sounded from the center of the smoky cloud, accompanied by a meaty thud.

Xandie's cousins ran to the edge of the smoke cloud and hauled out the still-bound Mathilde, dragging her out a back exit.

From the other side, Xandie searched for any sign of Elspeth. Low, rhythmic sobbing met her ears. She reached in and dragged out an unsteady Elspeth.

Emerging from the smoke, Xandie's grandmother coughed to clear her throat. She dropped her rope to the ground and kicked the chair away. "I really have to work on the odor aspect of those hexes. It smells worse than Lila's cookies in there."

Both women shuddered at the thought of Lila's cookies.

"I heard crying. Are you okay?"

"Almost forgot." Elspeth reached in and dragged a sobbing Simon out by the collar. "Half fae has no spine. Once the smoke hit, he lost it. One punch and he went down in tears. I'm so disappointed."

"My brother always had an issue with confrontation. That's why he has me." Sabine Germani moved out of the shadows with Charlie in tow. She held a sharp, silver knife to the normally perky woman's throat.

Xandie herded Elspeth and Simon out of the way. The smoke dissipated slightly. Enough so Xandie spotted an annoyed expression on Charlie's face.

"About time you turned up. I thought you were just going to leave your brother to suffer for your crimes by himself." Was always nice when a hunch played out.

"Please," Sabine scoffed. "Do not pretend you know about me."

"At first, no," Xandie admitted. "When I found the ledger in your van? *I knew.* I mean, come on. *Germani?*

Meaning of the Black Forest? How obvious did you want to be?"

Sabine pouted. "Humans are stupid. I thought I'd get away with it."

"You're half human. Your mother was a human. Remember?"

"How could I forget?" Sabine spat on the ground. Her hand tightened on the knife at Charlie's throat. "My mother, the plain vanilla human. No gifts. We both worked our whole life to make up for our father's mistake."

"And then the ring."

"That wasn't our grandfather's fault. That menace, Goldi Locks, stole the commission." Sabine bared her teeth. "Our grandfather raised us. Showed us what honor was. We owe him everything." Her eyes glowed a fanatical silver.

"We treated your family poorly. But that can be righted. You and your brother cannot restore your family's honor if you are incarcerated." Milly stepped forward, her lavender hair now silver and flowing down her back. The glasses had disappeared, and her eyes gleamed a sharp emerald. "Drop the knife, child. This is over."

Sabine shook her head. "I know who you are, Lady Greenhand. It's by your words the fae shunned us. You caused this."

Milly sighed and nodded. "You are correct, little one. My orders caused your shunning. But I was wrong. I would like to correct that right now." She held out her hand. "The knife, please."

"I don't think so. I'm better than you are. I think I'll keep the ring myself now." Sabine smirked. "Our grandfather will forget honor when we have power."

"What a shocker. All villains are greedy." Not a surprise to Xandie. What was a surprise was Milly's transformation into a noble fae. She hadn't seen that coming. Xandie whispered to her ring, "A little help right now." Green vines shot forward, wrapping around Sabine's ankles.

The ring gripped Xandie's finger and a wall of green surged from opposite sides of the tent, heading for Sabine.

The half fae stiffened, then hissed at Xandie, "I will kill her. Call off the room."

Biting her lip, Xandie clenched her hands into fists. The green wall and the vines slowly receded from Sabine's legs.

"I'm bored." Ignoring the knife, Charlie went limp in Sabine's arms, dragging the woman off balance. The perky juggler grabbed the killer's arm and flipped her over her shoulder.

With a moan, Sabine landed flat on her back, the thump hard enough that she released her knife.

Charlie kicked it to the side of the tent.

Elspeth cackled from the sidelines. "See? I'm not the only one who gets bored easily."

Colin bounded in, panting.

Eric stumbled in behind him a few seconds later, holding onto Nash's collar. "I couldn't stop them."

Xandie held up a hand. "It's okay. We've got it handled."

Colin sighed. "Aw man. I came to rescue my queen. I'm primed, ready for action."

"Save pet's family," the hellhound growled and jerked forward.

Eric let go of the hound's collar, but Nash had knocked him off balance and he collided with the pug.

Xandie scrabbled backward, heading for the exit, all thoughts of rescue and hostages gone in her haste to avoid the oncoming detonation.

"*Colin. No.*" Elspeth's wails echoed through the tent as Xandie shot out into the non-seafood scented air.

Murders solved. Hostages rescued, and Xandie had escaped the Colin bomb for once.

Life is good.

TWENTY-TWO

"Are you sure? From what I've observed, you're more than worthy of the ring."

Xandie nodded and extended her engagement ring to Milly, a.k.a. Lady Rosalind Greenhand. "I promised the ring if it helped, I'd return it to its owner. You might have to give it a good cleaning, though.

"If you allow me, I will have the amber stone that had originally been placed in this ring redesigned along with a replacement ring constructed in its place." She turned to a hovering henchman. "Tyr, surprisingly enough, has an amazing eye for design. Your new engagement ring will suit you perfectly."

Tyr pursed his lips. "I suppose, as my lady demands it, I could produce something passable for a Librarian."

Xandie snickered at Tyr's disgust. The supercilious man had grown on her. Particularly with his help the night before with the rescue. "Are you sure about Simon and Sabine?"

The noble nodded. "This was partially a fae-caused

problem. We shall help solve it. Their grandfather is awaiting them at my holdings. We will rehabilitate them all and restore their family honor."

"And Horace? Was he just cover?"

Blushing, Rosalind giggled. "Horace is a delight and has agreed to join me. He really is such a sweet man."

Standing behind his boss, Ty rolled his eyes at Xandie. Biting back her laughter, Xandie nodded with a smile. "Charlie has advised her bosses about the outcome of the rescue and that you're taking the Schwartzwalds back to fae land. The Paranormal Investigative Group isn't happy but have agreed to your jurisdiction in this matter."

Rosalind winked at Xandie. "As if PIG had a choice." She waved Tyr forward. "We have a gift for you."

Tyr shoved a takeaway cup of hot chocolate at Xandie. "From the bakery. Spelled to stay hot until you consume it. Enjoy."

Xandie accepted the drink with a smile. "Thank you."

"We must leave. Horace is waiting. But the various fae clans are pleased at how you handled the situation. We will be available if you ever need our assistance." Rosalind brushed a kiss over Xandie's cheek. "Take care, Librarian." The fae and her minion headed toward the Library door where she paused. "A rumor has come to my ears. A portent. Something is coming. Coming for the Harrows in Point Muse."

Xandie mimicked Tyr's earlier action and rolled her eyes. "Something is always coming for the Harrows."

"Not like this. This is a warring of blood. Of Harrow against Harrow. Be careful." She nodded to Xandie and disappeared out the door.

Shaking off the woman's warning, Xandie inhaled the

scent of the hot chocolate. She decided to take her beverage out to the back yard behind the Library. The sun had begun to set, bathing her yard in a beautiful orange glow. Xandie wandered to the edge of her bluff where a set of winding wooden stairs led down to the beach and a small dock...*and Elspeth Harrow.* "Why are you lurking outside my Library, Elspeth?" Xandie concentrated on her grandmother, her hot chocolate forgotten. A boat pulled up to the dock and a man climbed out. An elderly man with short gray hair stepped off, relying on a cane.

Elspeth stood to the side, her arms crossed, glaring.

The elderly man spoke a few words to Elspeth, who shook her head fiercely, denying whatever the other had said.

Xandie cursed the fact that she couldn't hear what the two were discussing, but it was obviously important enough for Elspeth to want to hide the meeting.

She moved as close as she dared toward the wooden stairs and strained to eavesdrop.

Elspeth continued ranting, waving a hand in the air.

The elderly gentleman from the boat seemed to stop listening and instead stared straight at Xandie. With familiar eyes. Amber colored eyes. Impossible eyes that occurred only in Harrow witches... Until now. The fae woman had been right.

Something is coming...

The end.

Want More?

You can sign up for my mailing list. It's for new releases and no spam. Be the first to grab specials, new releases, and freebies.

Sign up now

https://www.kellyethan.com/newsletter

LEAVE A REVIEW

Did you like this book?

Please leave a review for it on Amazon!

The Fiendish Foe and the Deadly Jewels

ABOUT THE AUTHOR

I want to thank everyone who spent the time to read my novel.

My world is small town magic, mystery and mayhem, with plenty of snarky laughs along the way.

With an overactive imagination and a love of all things that go bump in the night, it was natural to write cozy paranormal mysteries, but I also love paranormal romance. No matter the genre, I love sarcastic heroines who like to save the day and solve the puzzle.

With a busy and chaotic household, writing is my outlet for madness. I live in Australia and when not writing, I can be found plotting my next fictional murder or chasing after the family's ferocious hellhound.

Visit me today at my website or say hello on social media.

Website:
https://www.kellyethan.com

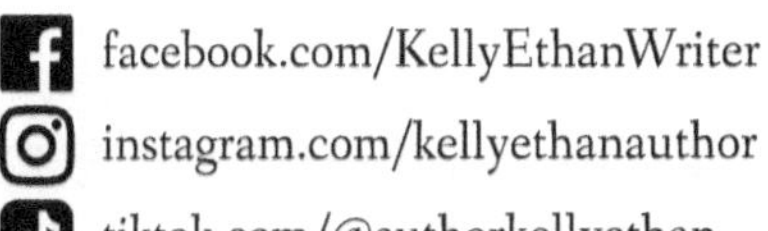

ALSO BY KELLY ETHAN

COZY PARANORMAL MYSTERY:

Point Muse Cozy Paranormal Mystery Series

The Wicked Witch and the Christmas Chaos
The Wicked Witch and the Stolen Snow Globe
The Conniving Carver and the Jeering Jack-O-Lantern
The Wicked Witch and the Ultimate Smackdown
The Wicked Witch and the Abominable Snowman
The Wicked Witch and the Killer Grinch

#0 The Pernicious Pixie and the Choked Word
#1 The Killer Knight and the Murderous Chairleg
#2 The Dastardly Dragon Killer and the Poisoned Breath
#3 The Murderous Monster and the Stony Gaze
#4 The Cursed Crow and the Deadly Hex
#5 The Slanderous Siren and the Grievous Gift
#6 The Vengeful Villain and the Cursed Treasure
#7 The Fiendish Foe and the Deadly Jewels
#8 The Nefarious Nemesis and the Wedding Jinx

Point Muse Cozy Paranormal Mystery Boxed Set: Books 1-3

Point Muse Cozy Paranormal Mystery Boxed Set: Books 4-6

Point Muse Cozy paranormal Mystery Boxed Set: Books 1-8

LILA HARROW: Point Muse Cozy Paranormal Mystery

Cookies, Curses and Christmas Corpses.

#1 Cupcakes, Corpses and Chaos

#2 Pies, Potions and Peril

#3 Sin, Sugar and Shadows

LILA HARROW Point Muse Boxed Set: Books 1-3

HOLLY HARROW: Point Muse Cozy Paranormal Mystery

Banshee, Vikings and Voodoo

#1 Banshee, Death and Disarray

#2 Banshee, Moonshine and Madness

#3 Banshee, Sea Monster and Sabotage

HOLLY HARROW Point Muse Boxed Set: Books 1-3

The Ghost Vein Mine Cozy Paranormal Mysteries

#1 Ghosts and Gold Dust

#2 Curses and Cold Cases

Non Fiction

Heart and Craft.